DECEPTION AT DARK HALL

Book Two of The Briony Martin Mystery Series

By

STACEY COVERSTONE

Copyright: 2013 by Stacey Coverstone
Cover Art by Sheri L. McGathy
Interior Layout by www.formatting4U.com
Visit Author's Website: www.staceycoverstone.com

This is a work of fiction. Names, characters, places, and incidents are either the product of the author's imagination or are used fictitiously, and any resemblance to actual persons living or dead, business establishments, events, or locales, is entirely coincidental.

All rights reserved. No part of this book may be used or reproduced in any manner whatsoever without written permission of the author.

DEDICATION

To my life partner, Paul

ACKNOWLEDGMENTS

Thank you to Melissa Blue and Mary Whealdon for reading, critiquing and editing this novella. Your assistance was greatly appreciated.

CHAPTER ONE

Early February 1956

Just over three months ago, Briony Martin bid farewell to the island of Cape Marble, Maine, its ghosts, and John Fletcher. Since she'd been back home in Kansas, John had called on the telephone once each week and they'd exchanged photos and monthly letters. But he'd yet to come visit as he'd promised the day the ferry chugged away from the dock.

She sat on the edge of her bed in the house she shared with her mother in Wichita. Every time she looked at the photo of John on her bedside table, an internal flame ignited. After he'd surprised her on Cape Marble's dock with a public and passionate kiss that had spoken of desire and possible love, Briony's heart soared with the promise of a potential future with the ruggedly handsome private investigator. Now it had been three consecutive weeks without word of any kind.

Releasing a sigh, she continued to pack clothes into the suitcase lying open on her bed.

Having succeeded in eradicating many of her former fears after returning to her quiet life as a court stenographer, Briony struggled to push down the building anxiety that bubbled. Although John had sworn his job mostly involved doing background checks, locating missing persons, conducting surveillance, and performing clandestine operations such as digging through people's trash and photographing cheating spouses, occasionally he found himself in dangerous situations dealing with hardened criminals.

Could one of those criminals have hurt him? Did he get injured while working on one of his cases? Was he sick and in the hospital? Or worse. Had he died? John's father passed away before Briony had a chance to meet him. There were no siblings. In the months they'd kept in touch, John hadn't mentioned the names of friends. There'd be no one to let her know if something terrible had happened to him.

Briony double-checked to make sure she had everything she needed for her trip and snapped the suitcase shut. Still reflecting, she pulled her winter jacket out of the closet and slipped her arms through.

After her father's abandonment and her brother Ben's death, she couldn't bear the thought of losing another person she loved. But there wasn't anything she could do aside from return to Maine and knock on John's door to see if he answered. If he answered, but his feelings for her had cooled or he'd found someone else, she'd be mortified. Besides, chasing after a man was not her way. Social norms were well defined. Dating rituals dictated the proper way for a man to court a woman—even long distance—and Briony was one to adhere to those rituals.

She was twenty-three and John was several years older. They were beyond pinning and going steady. But they'd grown close through the months. In her mind, their relationship had developed into something special. They'd exchanged more than photographs and letters; they'd shared heartfelt sentiments.

Glancing one more time at his photo, her breath hitched. At six feet tall with deep brown eyes, thick and wide sideburns, black hair styled in a pompadour, and an extroverted personality, John was unlike any man she'd ever known. She could see spending her life with him. At night before drifting to sleep, she even allowed herself the fantasy of imagining the day when he proposed marriage.

Would her fantasy become reality? Or were John's feelings for her only those of a good friend? Although he expressed warm affection, he hadn't told her he loved her. If he didn't care for her romantically, why waste both of their time with phone calls and promises of visits?

She wanted to believe he was an honorable man. But doubt as to his true intentions was beginning to creep into her bones like the icy chills she'd felt each time she encountered a ghost on Cape Marble.

Briony heaved the suitcase off of her bed and padded down the stairs. Even if she were a bold woman who didn't care what people thought, she still couldn't go to Maine. Her best friend, Paige, had invited her to Chicago to meet her new baby, Amanda. Briony was the godmother, and Paige wanted her there for the baby's christening.

Because the bus ride would be more than eleven hours and too much time to spare, she was flying on an airplane for the first time. The two-hour flight on TWA would land at Chicago Midway, the world's busiest airport. That in itself made her heart pound.

When she saw her mother waiting at the kitchen door to drive her to the Wichita Mid-Continent Airport, a knot twisted her stomach. Concerns that the plane might run out of fuel, lose an engine, or crash momentarily diverted her thoughts of John.

"We'd better get a move on," her mother said, checking her wristwatch. "You might miss your flight if there's traffic."

Although Briony was anxious to spend five days of quality time with Paige, her husband Mark and their baby, she questioned the decision to take an airplane rather than a bus. But her mother, who'd become a happier and more carefree person since finding closure regarding her missing husband, had encouraged her to continue on her journey of trying new things.

You'll be all right, Briony told herself. *Airplanes are as safe as cars. That's what the advertisements say.* She slid onto the seat of the family Buick and began deep breathing as her mother backed out of the driveway and pressed on the gas.

~ * ~

She survived the flight and discovered she'd enjoyed the experience. Even in winter, Chicago from the air had been a beautiful sight.

"I'm so glad you were able to come," Paige said, sitting across from Briony at her chrome kitchen table. Briony cradled a hot mug of tea in her palms. It was just what she needed to take the chill off. As soon as she'd stepped out of the airport terminal and into Paige and Mark's waiting car, the sky had opened up to release a freezing rain, and it hadn't let up.

Once they'd reached the Collier's two-story brick house on a tree-lined street, Paige put Amanda down for a nap, and Mark made himself scarce to allow the friends time to catch up.

"I wouldn't have missed my goddaughter's christening for anything," Briony said. "And I've missed you so much. A year is too long between visits." She squeezed Paige's hand. "Amanda is adorable. In fact, I don't think I've ever seen a more perfect child."

Paige smiled. "Thank you. She's a good baby, too. Rarely does she cry. She takes after her father. Mark is a laid-back person, you know."

"He looks content. You both do. Marriage and relocating, and now parenthood, seems to agrees with you." It was just a little over one year ago that Briony had been the maid of honor at Paige and Mark's wedding. They moved shortly afterward to Chicago for a job opportunity for him. Paige had worked at a cosmetics counter in a department store before getting pregnant.

"Do you miss working?" Briony asked. She liked her job as a court stenographer, but assumed she'd give it up when the time came that she married and had a child of her own.

Paige shook her head. "You know I only worked to pass the time until we conceived. I always wanted to be a wife and mother. I'm satisfied being at home with Amanda. In my opinion, raising a child is the most important job a woman can hold."

"I couldn't agree more." Briony smiled and sipped at her drink, sorry that her own mother had been forced to work outside the home when Briony's father abandoned his family. She glanced around Paige's kitchen to admire the matching avocado appliances, gingham curtains at the window, a rooster clock hanging on one wall, and an oversized fork and spoon on another. "Your house is cute. It must be fun to decorate it the way you want."

Paige chuckled. "I do enjoy domesticity. Mark and I have a modern marriage in which our duties are divided equally. I shop and he pays the bills."

They both laughed.

"Enough about me for now," Paige said, leaning forward. Her eyes twinkled with mischief. "I want to hear all about you. Tell me more about this mystery man of yours, John Fletcher. You've been so cagey on the phone when talking about him."

It'd been far too long since they'd shared secrets and dreams with one another in person. Talking on the phone wasn't the same. When Briony first returned from Maine, she'd called and told Paige about her cross-country trip and explained how she'd learned her father had been murdered, and how the murderer had almost killed her, too. She'd even revealed her experiences with the ghosts in the lighthouse. John's name had come up casually, and Paige had said she'd been able to tell from the lilt in Briony's voice that he was special. Now she wanted the juicy details.

Briony finished sharing her unease about not hearing from John for three weeks when the kitchen door opened. A man looking vaguely familiar rushed in, slammed the door behind him, and wiped his wet shoes on the doormat. Water dripped from his coattails and rolled off the brim of his gray fedora.

"It's still raining cats and dogs," he said, glancing

between Briony and Paige.

"Sit down and I'll pour you a cup of tea. It'll warm you up." Paige scooted her chair out from under the table and stepped toward the stove.

He hung his jacket and hat on a peg by the door. "Don't bother. I'm going to take a hot shower. No need to set a place for me at dinner either. I'm going out tonight."

"Before dinner?" Paige looked disappointed.

"I'll grab something at the diner down the street."

"Going to Dark Hall again?" Paige's eyebrow arched.

"Yes, I am." His gaze narrowed, and then his head jerked toward Briony. The tight lines of his mouth relaxed and formed a polite smile. Stepping forward, he held out his hand. "Forgive my rudeness, Miss Martin. Paige and Mark told me you were coming. Nice to see you again."

She shook his hand and stared, wondering how he knew her.

"Don't you remember Mark's brother, Daniel?" Paige asked. "You met at our wedding."

That was where she'd seen him. "Of course. I thought you looked familiar."

"I guess I didn't make that big of an impression," he teased. "You're here for the christening."

"Yes. I wouldn't have missed it for the world." Briony suddenly remembered Paige telling her that she and Mark had chosen his brother as another godparent. "You and I are fortunate to have been selected as godparents for such a precious little treasure as Amanda," she said to him.

"I just hope I'll be able to live up to the obligation

involved."

"Of course you will," Paige said.

Obviously distracted, he skimmed a hand through his disheveled hair and glanced at the rooster clock. "If you'll both excuse me, I'm going to say hello to Mark and then shower and change. Mark's home, isn't he, Paige?"

"In the living room," she said.

He nodded. "See you both later."

When he left the kitchen and was out of earshot, Paige returned to her seat. A gray pallor replaced her previously sunny expression.

"What's wrong?" Briony asked. She could read her friend like a book.

Paige's voice lowered to a whisper. "It's Daniel. I'm worried about him. Mark is, too."

"Worried? About what?"

"It's this woman he's been seeing. We think she's a bad influence on him."

"I didn't even know Daniel lived in Chicago. When did that happen?"

"He moved here shortly after we did. Unfortunately, he was laid off from his job in St. Louis. Mark thought a change would do him good so he helped him find a position here. So far it's working out."

"Oh. You say he's seeing a woman? In what way is she a bad influence?"

Paige's gaze shifted to the doorway. Daniel and Mark's conversation could easily be heard from the kitchen. Her voice was barely audible when she answered. "Mark and I believe she could be into witchcraft and drugs, and God knows what else.

Daniel has changed since he met her."

Briony felt her eyes widen. "Witchcraft and drugs? Where did he meet this woman?"

"At a séance."

"What?" At an outward glance, Daniel Collier appeared to be as straight as an arrow. She couldn't imagine him attending a séance.

Paige nodded. "The woman's name is Sharlyn Dark. She lives in a Victorian mansion downtown called Dark Hall. She's a medium, and she holds séances in the mansion."

"Do you mean she speaks to the dead?"

"That's her claim." Paige rolled her eyes. "Daniel and a few of the people he works with got into a discussion one day about life after death. None of his co-workers knew about his fiancé, Monica. She died four months ago right before their wedding. He's kept his pain to himself. But he apparently blurted out the story that day and mentioned he'd do anything to see Monica's face or hear her voice one more time. He met Monica soon after he moved here to Chicago, and they fell in love quickly. Her death shattered him."

Briony sighed. "So sad. Although I didn't initially recognize Daniel, I do remember a phone conversation in which you mentioned his fiancé. What a tragedy. She suffered a brain aneurism, if I recall correctly."

"That's right. Anyway, one of Daniel's co-workers had been to Dark Hall, and he invited Daniel to go with him a few weeks ago to attend a séance. That's when Daniel met Sharlyn Dark. He came home claiming Monica had made her presence known, and she'd spoken to him through Miss Dark. I hadn't seen him so animated and full of life since before Monica's passing. He's gone back two or three times a week since. He seems to be obsessed—or perhaps *possessed.*"

Briony had heard of these types of scam artists. There had been a similar court case in Wichita, in which a woman sued a self-proclaimed psychic on behalf of her elderly mother. The daughter claimed the psychic tricked her mother into giving her jewelry and money, and even named her in her will! Briony had been the court stenographer and found the case both disturbing and fascinating.

"Does Daniel live here with you and Mark?" she asked.

"After Monica's death, he was unable to step foot inside the house he'd bought for the two of them. There was no way he could afford both a mortgage and an apartment lease, so we let him move in temporarily while he tried to sell the house. A couple has finally signed a contract, so hopefully, he'll be able to afford his own place soon."

From across the table, Briony patted Paige's hand. "Why didn't you tell me he was staying here? I could have reserved a motel room. In fact, I'm sure I can find a motel close by and take a taxi back and forth. With the new baby and the christening coming up, you have far too much going on right now to bother with another person in the house."

Paige would have none of it. "Don't be ridiculous. We have two spare rooms. The baby stays in our bedroom with us for now. I want you here. You're my best friend. But I apologize for not telling you on the phone about Daniel. Are you going to be uncomfortable with him around?"

"No, of course not. He's Mark's brother and seems like a nice enough fellow. But are you sure it won't be too much for you?"

Paige stood up and hugged Briony around the shoulders. Tears sparkled in her eyes. "I'm positive. I'm so happy you're here."

"So am I. Of course, I'll help with cooking or cleaning, or whatever you need."

Paige smiled and took her seat again.

"What makes you think this medium is into witchcraft and drugs?" Briony asked, returning to the subject.

"Mark did some subtle asking around. There are rumors, and Daniel has been acting strange. He comes home from Dark Hall with glassy eyes and smelling like fruity tobacco, but he doesn't smoke. Or, at least, he didn't smoke before. He's become more irritable and snaps if Mark or I ask him any questions about Miss Dark or what's going on at her mansion."

"Do you know if he pays a reading fee each time he attends a séance?"

"He does, although I don't know how much. He slipped up once and mentioned something to that effect and then clamped his mouth shut. He knows Mark wouldn't approve of him throwing his money away."

Briony told her about the case she'd worked on in Wichita and suggested Daniel might be the victim of a scam. "Has Mark ever gone to the mansion with Daniel to meet Miss Dark?"

"No. He's been too busy with work and helping me with the baby. And Daniel's his older brother. Mark doesn't want to step on his toes, although he's as worried about the situation as I am. We don't know what to do. Daniel's heart was broken when Monica died. He's still vulnerable. We hate to think someone is taking advantage of him, or he's trying to stave off his sadness by using drugs."

Briony had never seen Paige's face so wrought with worry. "I wish there was something I could do to help," she said.

"There might be," Paige replied quickly. "Would you go with Daniel to Dark Hall and see for yourself what this woman is up to? After your experiences in Maine with investigating your father's murder and communing with ghosts, you seem the perfect person to be able to figure out if Daniel's in danger or not."

Briony leaned back in her chair. "Wait a minute. I'm not a detective, and I know nothing about mediums."

"But you know about scam artists. You just said so. And you have good intuition. Please, Briony. If you sense something fishy is going on, maybe you can talk some sense into Daniel whereas Mark and I can't. Or if you can determine this woman, Sharlyn Dark, is doing something illegal, like selling him drugs or coercing him into giving her his money, we can go to the police."

Briony wished John was here. He was the real detective. He'd know how to interrogate someone correctly and search for clues without being obvious. He did a great job doing just that on Cape Marble. An idea skated through her mind. Perhaps he could give her advice over the phone. This could be the perfect excuse for her to call him.

"Please, Briony," Paige begged. "Daniel is Mark's

only sibling. If he were to end up arrested, broke, addicted, or part of a cult or something, we'd never forgive ourselves for not stepping in. We want to help, but he won't listen to us."

Briony shrugged her shoulders. "What makes you think he'd listen to any words of wisdom I'll have to offer? I'm no one to him."

"That's just it," Paige said with enthusiasm. "I'm sure you've heard that old adage about how it's easier for someone to share his deepest secrets with a stranger. With you, Daniel will have less fear of being judged. He might feel free to be honest and more likely to listen to your advice."

Briony gazed into Paige's pleading eyes and couldn't say no. She'd thought she was coming to Chicago to take her mind off of John, spend some down time with her best friend, and to participate in her goddaughter's christening. It seemed a séance in a Victorian mansion would be part of the itinerary as well.

CHAPTER TWO

Daniel's gaze ping-ponged between Mark and Paige and then landed on Briony. Obviously, he was confused as to why a woman he'd met only once before now would want to go to a séance with him tonight rather than stay at home visiting with her best friend whom she hadn't seen in over a year. Briony didn't blame him for acting suspicious. She thought the plan bordered on absurd and would probably backfire on them, but she'd do anything for Paige.

"Aren't you tired from traveling?" he asked her.

"No, I feel fine. The flight wasn't long. The trip was exhilarating. In fact, my adrenaline is still flowing." That was the truth. But she really had no desire to go out into the cold rain, meet a strange woman, and participate in a séance. She'd rather enjoy conversation with Paige and Mark over dinner and coo at the baby all evening.

"Briony had some unusual experiences not long ago when she was in Maine," Paige revealed. "She saw ghosts. One of them interceded when she was about to be murdered."

Briony couldn't believe Paige just said that. She pursed her lips and shot her friend a look that implied she had a big mouth. Mark didn't appear surprised, so Paige had evidently shared Briony's secret with her husband. Daniel, however, took notice. His interest suddenly grew.

"Really? So you believe in communicating with spirits from beyond."

"Uh, yes. Now I do."

"I'm curious about your experience in Maine. Whose ghosts did you encounter?"

Briony swallowed and glanced at Paige, who nodded her encouragement to go on. "Let's see. There was a girl named Sally, some babies who had passed over, a woman named Mira—she's the one who saved my life—and my father."

Daniel's eyes enlarged. "Did you talk to your father? Was he able to speak?"

She nodded. "He materialized in front of me and yes, he spoke. He apologized for causing our family grief many years ago, and he asked for forgiveness."

A smile quirked the corner of Daniel's mouth. Then his smug gaze moved from Mark to Paige. "Will you believe me now when I tell you Monica has been communicating with me through Sharlyn? Your friend just confirmed there are supernatural occurrences that take place in this world, even if you don't understand how they happen."

Neither Paige nor Mark commented. Their faces looked made of stone, and the silence was awkward. Briony felt compelled to address his remark. For Paige and Mark's sakes, she hoped to further convince Daniel to let her tag along tonight.

"When Paige told me about Dark Hall, I became excited and asked if I might finagle an invitation to go with you. Ever since my experiences in Maine, I've been fascinated by the paranormal and have even considered visiting a medium. But I haven't found the courage to go alone. This seems like the perfect opportunity."

Daniel urged her to continue. "Is there someone else, aside from your father, you'd like to communicate with?"

She cleared her throat and felt a quickening in her chest. "Paige probably hasn't mentioned it, but I had a twin brother, Ben. He passed away five years ago. I'm wondering if Miss Dark might be able to invoke his spirit."

The words spilled from her mouth without thought and before realizing what she was saying. She studied the myriad emotions that crossed Daniel's face and felt stirrings within her own body. She sensed her twin was always with her, but never had she considered conjuring him up from the other world. A prickly feeling niggled beneath goose-fleshed skin at the thought.

Daniel smiled broadly. "I'd be pleased for you to go with me tonight. I'm sure Sharlyn—Miss Dark—won't mind another guest."

Briony heard the exhalation of breath that Paige probably didn't know she'd been holding. The two women exchanged a cunning glance.

When Paige asked Daniel to reconsider staying for dinner before heading out to Dark Hall, he relented. "I should have realized she's planned something special for your first night in Chicago."

"Yes, I have," Paige announced, "and it'll be much better than a greasy burger. I'm glad you've decided to join us." She grinned. "Dinner will be ready in an hour." She winked at Briony and then set about pulling pots and pans out of the metal cabinets.

~ * ~

The rain had tapered to a slow drizzle by the time Briony and Daniel set off for Dark Hall in his older Dodge Coronet. Along the drive, he pointed out a few city landmarks, but he didn't converse beyond his narration as a tour guide. However, once they reached North Lake Shore Drive, she sensed a change in his mood. He became more animated and somewhat giddy.

He mentioned that it had taken three years to build Dark Hall. Construction had begun in 1882 and finished in 1885. "Sharlyn's ancestor, Palmer Dark, built the mansion for him and his wife to use for social gatherings. They entertained many famous people of the time, including the former U.S. President Ulysses S. Grant. Palmer had been a prominent businessman who was responsible for much of the development of State Street. At the time, Dark Hall was the largest private residence in Chicago. The construction of the mansion, which faces Lake Michigan on Lake Shore Drive, established the Gold Coast neighborhood. It's still one of the most affluent neighborhoods in the city. Be prepared to be bowled over," he said, smiling.

Daniel wasn't kidding. Briony looked through the windshield and gasped.

As he turned off the street and drove through a wrought iron gate with brick pillars on each side, her mouth dropped open. Up ahead was a three-story mansion built of stone that looked more like a European castle with its many turrets and minarets.

"Pretty spectacular, isn't it?" he said.

She was stunned beyond words.

He stopped the car in the circular driveway in front of the manor. Two men dressed in gray coats and billed caps appeared at each of their respective doors. The one standing at the passenger side opened the door and assisted Briony out by the hand.

The other valet bowed and then opened the door for Daniel and outstretched his palm. "Good evening, Mr. Collier."

Daniel placed his car keys in the man's hand. "Good evening, Dawson."

Briony noticed the subtle change in Daniel's voice, and even the adjustment of his posture once he was outside the vehicle.

"Have a good evening, Mr. Collier," the valet said, nodding.

"Thank you, Dawson."

The valet folded his long body into Daniel's Dodge, pressed upon the gas pedal, and disappeared around the corner with the vehicle.

Daniel stepped toward Briony and offered her his arm. "Everything at Dark Hall is high class. Sharlyn's ancestors knew how to properly entertain, and she has continued their traditions. It's all in the breeding, as you'll see when you meet her."

He appeared to have transformed from a typical middle class man with a seven-year-old car to a fellow of culture, simply by walking into the shadow of the Gothic mansion. Briony's head angled when she realized the mansion's massive outside door had been constructed without a lock and knob.

Daniel followed her gaze and chuckled. "The only

way to get into Dark Hall is to be admitted from the inside. Wealthy people can't be too careful." He pushed a buzzer next to the door. When a voice crackled through an intercom speaker, he gave their names. "Daniel Collier and Miss Martin here for the séance."

The door creaked open a moment later and an unsmiling butler in full regalia admitted them. Briony found herself squeezing Daniel's arm a little too tightly. The setting was straight out of a Gothic novel, and the mansion seemed cold and unwelcoming, especially on a rainy March evening.

Something Paige had said ran through her mind quickly. One of Paige's concerns was that Daniel might be handing over significant amounts of his hard-earned money to this woman, Miss Dark. As Briony stepped into the three-story central hall that had been built under a glass dome and had a spiral staircase rising eighty feet into the tower without a center support, that theory flew out the window. There was no way Sharlyn Dark needed anyone's money. The place resembled a museum or a European castle more than a home. However, just because someone was rich, she reasoned, that didn't mean they didn't need or crave more.

"Wait here," said the butler in a monotone voice. He took their jackets and vanished down a dimly lit hallway.

"This place is incredible," Briony whispered, glancing at the ornate tapestries and portraits hanging on the surrounding walnut paneled walls.

Daniel whispered back. "I've been given a tour of the entire mansion. There are rooms finished in a variety of historic styles. There's a Louis the sixteenth salon, an Indian room, an Ottoman parlor, a Renaissance library, a Spanish music room, an English dining room that seats fifty, and a Moorish study; the rugs of which are saturated with perfumes. Paintings collected by the original Mrs. Dark adorn the grand ballroom, which is seventy-five feet long and has a marble floor."

"I take it Miss Dark doesn't hold séances because she needs the income," Briony said, tongue in cheek, but also to check his reaction.

Daniel's face seemed petrified into a strange expression of wonderment. "Sharlyn does it because she's been blessed with a gift, Briony. She's selfless. It's her only wish to help people connect with those they love that have passed on."

"You may follow me now," the butler said, appearing from the depths of the gloomy hall like a phantom and interrupting their conversation.

The two of them trailed him down a different hall and into another corridor. They were escorted onto an elevator, which took them to the second floor. Upon exiting the elevator, the butler led them down still another hallway and up a short set of stairs that were covered with red carpet the shade of blood. By the time they were finally shown into a room, Briony's heart was in her throat.

The room they entered was small, carpeted, and paneled in more rich wood. It smelled strongly of the musky scent of patchouli. Dimly lit by what appeared to be electric wall sconces, the lamps seemed to be set on their lowest wattage. At the far end of the room sat a large round table. Seated around the table were four people, none of whom were talking. The room was as quiet as a tomb.

Daniel escorted Briony to the table. All eyes turned to stare at them when they approached. His voice delved low to match the somber quality of the atmosphere when he introduced her to the others.

"This is Miss Briony Martin from Wichita, Kansas. She's here visiting my brother and sister-in-law."

The bobbing of heads and soft murmurs welcomed her. She noticed Daniel's gaze had locked on the woman sitting at the head of the table. Above her on the wall was a huge ancient looking tapestry woven with muted colors. As Briony's gaze moved over it, a shudder sliced through her. The unsettling scene portrayed a nude woman with long flowing hair standing under a full moon. A half dozen rams with curled horns, cloven hooves, and flared nostrils surrounded her. The woman's eyes were closed, and her mouth was open in what appeared to be a cry; of agony or ecstasy, Briony wasn't sure which. Either way, the picture was troubling. She wondered what would possess anyone to purchase such a horrid piece. Maybe Paige and Mark were onto something after all, with regard to the witchcraft rumors.

Daniel's voice interrupted her musings. "Briony, I'd like to introduce you to Miss Sharlyn Dark."

Her gaze shifted away from the tapestry. Miss Dark, whom she guessed to be in her early twenties, was stunningly beautiful. Her heart-shaped face was as pale as a winter's moon and seemed to be filled with an unearthly glow. Strawberry blonde hair cascaded down her shoulders in ripples. Her lips were full and rosy, her eyebrows light and feathery, and her ice blue eyes were almond shaped, adding to her otherworldly quality. Although a shawl was draped around her shoulders, Briony could tell she was petite and fine boned. Under the shawl she wore pale pink. If wings protruded from her back, she'd look like a virginal fairy.

Briony glanced at Daniel again. His eyes seemed to be glazed over with the look of...what was it? Respect? Admiration? Or could he be in love with the woman?

Although their hostess was as mysterious and beguiling of a creature that Briony had ever met, it was Miss Dark's eyes that enraptured her the most. The young woman looked directly at her, yet her gaze seemed to be looking just below eye level, as if through her, perhaps into her soul. It crossed Briony's mind that maybe she *could* see somewhere beyond where others could not.

"It's a pleasure to have you join us," Miss Dark said. Her voice was as lovely as the rest of her—sweet and bewitching. She nodded, and the wisp of a smile crinkled her lips. Then her left hand touched the sleeve of the person standing next to her. "This is Lee, my assistant."

It was then that Briony took note of the young man. Miss Dark and the ugly tapestry had captured her full attention. She hadn't noticed Lee until now. Slender and short in stature, his hair was platinum blond, like many of the female movie stars of the day, and parted on the side. Unsmiling, his nose was pert, and his eyes were as gray as a foggy morning. The way he stared gave Briony the feeling that he was always on guard and distrustful. The poor boy's ears were too large for his head, giving him a comical appearance. However, it was apparent that he took his job as assistant to Miss Dark seriously. His pinstriped suit was gray, spotless, and ironed perfectly. A crisp white shirt and black tie finished the outfit to give him a professional and distinguished flair.

"Say hello to our guests, Lee," Miss Dark directed.

He cleared his throat and said, "Hello. Thank you for coming. We're pleased to have all of you tonight." His head bowed toward each of the guests, including Briony and Daniel.

Something about the young man suddenly bothered her. His voice seemed too high. When he swept his tongue across his bottom lip, she felt the hairs on her arms stand on end. Her gaze narrowed, and she noticed the delicate curve of his jaw, the slimness of his shoulders, and plucked eyebrows. Her inquisitive gaze traveled to his throat. Lee had no Adam's apple. The revelation struck her like lightning. Lee was not a man. She was a woman dressed like a man! But why? Briony felt her own eyebrows snap together in wonderment. No wonder Paige was so worried about her brother-in-law. This was a strange house indeed.

"What are you wearing tonight, Miss Martin?" Miss Dark asked.

Briony was briefly taken aback by the question. Although the room was dim, she was standing across from the woman. Couldn't she see what she was wearing? Anyway, why did it matter? Fishing for personal information probably had something to do with her scam. Miss Dark's mystical eyes nearly glowed as she stared through and beyond Briony. Once again, she felt a chill like the brush of spider webs across her back. It was then that she understood. Sharlyn Dark was blind.

Due to the bizarre nature of the evening thus far, Briony momentarily forgot what she was wearing. She glanced down at her outfit and answered quietly. "I'm in a knee-length skirt, a white blouse, and a green sweater."

"She also has a beautiful silk scarf tied around her neck," Daniel added.

"And your hair and eyes?" Miss Dark inquired. "What color are they?"

"Brown."

Briony was about to ask why that information was needed when Miss Dark said, "Thank you. Please take your seats, and we'll begin." She nodded, and Lee lowered himself (or rather, herself) into the chair next to her.

Daniel pulled out the empty chair next to Lee. Briony smoothed her skirt beneath her thighs, and Daniel scooted her in and then took the seat next to her. When Briony glanced at Miss Dark again, the woman's gaze remained fixed straight ahead though she tilted her head slightly in Briony's direction. A gasp caught in her throat. Miss Dark *was* blind, wasn't she?

"We will begin," their hostess announced.

The light flickering off the wall sconces lowered even further, as if on their own, throwing the room into near total darkness. Briony heard the shallow breaths of Daniel on one side of her and the stifled breathing of the older woman at her other shoulder. When her eyes adjusted to the dim, she strained to see Miss Dark in the shadows opposite her. The self-proclaimed medium's own eyes were closed. She began to gently sway to the beat of a rhythm only she could hear.

As Briony nonchalantly glanced at the others around the table, she saw their eyes were all closed, too. Everyone, except her, seemed relaxed. No doubt they eagerly anticipated the spectacle to come. She wondered. Whose spirits would be summoned tonight? Men? Women? Children? Although her heart was jumping, she rather looked forward to hearing Miss Dark's impersonations and trying to determine how she accomplished the charade. She let her eyes drift shut.

Ten long minutes passed in dead silence without an utter from Miss Dark's mouth. Though the temptation was strong, Briony resisted the urge to shift in her seat. It seemed as if no one else had moved a muscle. Another five minutes passed. She allowed one eye to slowly wink open. Everyone else remained still as statues with their eyes closed.

The tension of remaining perfectly quiet for yet another five minutes was almost more than Briony could bear. She wished a phantom trumpet would blare or chains would rattle, or a ghost would groan. If a door slammed shut on its own, at least someone might scream or leapt from his or her chair. Anything to get the party going, she thought, with a noiseless sigh.

Suddenly, the air in the room crackled with static electricity. A low moan escaped Miss Dark's lips. "Who is there?" she called out. "Who calls me from the grave? Come forth, Spirit. Come forth and speak to this assembly."

Briony's gaze shifted between Sharlyn and Lee in order to determine if they would be working together somehow to fool the audience. Lee remained stiff and still. Miss Dark's eyelids flipped open, and her head turned to the woman sitting at her right. Then her rosy lips parted, and her voice came out small. "Mother, it is I, Albert. Can you hear me?"

The woman gasped. Her fist covered her mouth and tears burst from her eyes and rolled down her powdered cheeks. "Yes, Albert. I hear you. Is it really you, my precious son?"

"It is, Mother," Sharlyn answered in a young boy's voice. "I've missed you so. Have you missed me?"

"More than you could ever know," the woman blubbered.

Briony listened as mother and son carried on a short conversation. Albert ended by assuring her that the light was beautiful and he was being taken care of by his grandparents.

Shortly afterward, another spirit spoke. This time Sharlyn's voice deepened to a baritone. Apparently, he was the uncle of the stocky, whiskered man at the table. He had a message for his brother. "Lyndon," Sharlyn's voice boomed, "tell your father that I forgive him for what happened in the summer of 1948. He'll understand. Do you hear what I say? I won't rest until he knows I don't hold him responsible."

Lyndon mopped his forehead with a hankie and promised to deliver the message to his father.

Next, the woman sitting next to Briony was gifted

with a visit from her recently departed mother. She and Sharlyn (speaking as her mother) discussed topics such as the roses in her garden, her jewelry that she wished to be divided between family members, and the assurance that she no longer suffered.

As Briony raptly listened and watched the interactions, she realized just how lonely and desperate these people must be. She couldn't fathom how intelligent men and women could believe voices from beyond the grave were able to speak through this young blind woman. Although she didn't know how to prove it, Briony was sure Miss Dark was performing nothing more than a parlor trick. The darkened room, overwhelming scents, and strange surroundings added to the deception.

She stared at Daniel. His face was stretched tight with expectation. It was obvious he hoped to hear from his beloved fiancé. But what if Monica didn't show herself tonight? How would he react? Would he be devastated?

Briony bristled in her seat as both the emotional and physical strain in her body prepared to uncoil. How dare Miss Dark dupe these poor folks into thinking they were communicating with their loved ones. If it wasn't for money, what did she have to gain by this sham?

Her mind was wandering and contemplating the puzzle when Miss Dark looked straight at her. She grinned and said, "Briony, I'm so happy to see you. It's been such a long time."

Briony's thoughts snapped into the here and now.

"Don't you recognize me?" Miss Dark angled her head. Her voice had once more changed, this time to a more masculine tone, though not as rough and overbearing as the impersonation she'd done of Lyndon's uncle. Her eyes twinkled with mischief, and she tugged on her earlobe.

The hairs on the back of Briony's neck stiffened. That gesture was a familiar one. Although she knew all of this was a trick, it seemed the world stopped spinning for a moment. She felt Daniel's steady gaze on her.

"Do you know the voice?" he whispered.

She inhaled deeply, but didn't answer. Her gaze remained locked on Miss Dark's. The young woman stared at her with those ice blue eyes. Then they suddenly rolled up into her head. Her next words resonated in a plea. "Please acknowledge me, Briony. We have so much to talk about. Mother…father… I know you spoke to him. He asked for your forgiveness."

She felt the color drain from her face. Her mouth grew as dry as sawdust.

"Aren't you going to answer the boy?" asked Lee, with a hint of aggravation.

Briony shook her head. It was true she'd seen and spoken to the ghost of her father in Maine. But this was different. The dead couldn't speak through the living. It had to be a hoax.

Beside her, she could sense Daniel's agitation. "Who is it?" he asked.

Before she could answer, Sharlyn's hand smacked the wooden table, causing her and the woman next to her to jump. Miss Dark's peculiar unattached voice thundered out the answer. "Say something, Briony. Don't be afraid. Tell them I'm your brother Ben."

CHAPTER THREE

Briony couldn't breathe. She shoved away from the table and stood on wobbling legs. "Excuse me, but I can't stay here. I need air." She turned on her heel and scurried toward the door.

Daniel leaped from his seat and followed her out of the room. When they stepped into the hushed hallway, the stone-faced butler appeared like magic.

"Shall I retrieve your coats?" he asked.

"Yes," Daniel replied, with a curt nod.

Briony reached for calm by taking several deep breaths. When her quickened pulse slowed to a steadier rate, she touched Daniel's arm. "I hate for you to leave on my account. I don't mean to ruin your evening. Go back inside. I can wait downstairs or in the car until the séance is over."

His gaze was sympathetic, which she was grateful for. "Don't be silly. I can come to Dark Hall anytime. I'll be glad to take you home now, if you'd like."

"Are you sure?"

"Positive." His words were genuine even if his smile was taut.

"All right then. Perhaps it would be better. I'm suddenly feeling quite tired."

"Follow me," the butler said. After showing them into the same elevator and then winding them through the maze of assorted hallways, she and Daniel found themselves on the ground floor in the foyer standing under the glass dome. The butler disappeared and returned with their jackets several moments later. He flipped the locking mechanism on the inside of the massive front door and let them out with the friendliness of a cold fish.

The temperature had dropped. Wishing she was wearing a hat and scarf, Briony wrapped her arms around herself as a frigid wind cut through her. Daniel pulled a pack of cigarettes from his pocket and lit one up. She recalled Paige telling her he didn't smoke. What else did her best friend not know about her brother-in-law?

The Coronet appeared from around the corner within moments. The same valet who had driven it away earlier parked it in the circular driveway in front of them and jumped out of the driver's seat. Daniel flicked the cigarette into the gravel and stubbed it out with the toe of his shoe.

The valet first opened the passenger car door for Briony. Then he jogged around to Daniel's side and opened that door. "Good night, Mr. Collier," he said, tipping his cap as Daniel entered the vehicle.

"Good night, Dawson. Thank you."

Briony saw him stuff a bill into the valet's hand.

"Thank you, Mr. Collier."

As Daniel drove through the gate and into the street, she realized he'd left Dark Hall without giving Sharlyn Dark any money. Perhaps she'd send an invoice.

The streets were dark and deserted on the return drive to Paige and Mark's house. Like a gentleman, Daniel allowed her time to regain her composure. He waited until they were almost to the house before breaking the silence between them. He asked why she'd gotten upset at hearing her brother's voice. "I thought you went with me tonight hoping to make contact with him."

She could hardly tell Daniel she'd gone only as a favor to Paige and to try to somehow convince him that Miss Dark may not be what she seemed. But she was tired and confused as to what had occurred. She didn't want to explain anything right now—not her motive for going to Dark Hall in the first place, nor the unsettling feeling in her stomach that had caused her to flee from that room.

Had her twin really made contact with her through Miss Dark? Briony had no idea. But the truth was that the blind woman spooked her. There was no way she could have known Briony had a brother or that he'd died five years ago. The only possible explanation was that Daniel had called her ahead of time and told her about Ben.

She stared at his profile and wondered what his motive would be in doing such a thing. But more than his possible duplicity, it was that gesture—the tugging of the earlobe—that caused her alarm. "I'd rather not discuss it, if you don't mind," she answered, hoping he'd be polite enough to drop the subject. He was.

When they entered through the unlocked back door of the Collier home, Paige met them in the kitchen. She slid a finger to her lips.

"Shhh. Mark and the baby are both asleep already."

Daniel hung his hat on the peg next to the door. Then he whispered good night to both of them and strode out of the kitchen before Paige could ask him any questions. His room was evidently on the first level. Briony heard his footsteps cross the living room floor and then the click of a closing door.

"Well. What did you discover about Dark Hall and that woman?" Paige asked quietly. Her eyes lit up with curiosity.

Briony sighed. "Dark Hall is a strange place. The good news is that I didn't see any signs of drug use. The room where the séance was held smelled of patchouli, however. Daniel has probably brought the scent home on his clothes, which is most likely the reason you've thought he's been smoking something illegal. Also, Miss Dark has an assistant by the name of Lee that appears to be a man but is actually a woman. I'm not sure if Daniel knows that or not."

Paige's eyes widened. "How odd."

"And there's a weird tapestry hanging on the wall where the séance was conducted." She described it.

"That sounds perverted." Paige wrinkled her nose. "It could be symbolic of witchcraft, don't you think?"

"I suppose."

"Did the woman make poor Daniel think he was speaking to Monica again?"

"No, but she did *conjure* up the relatives of several other people in attendance." She used air quotes when she said the word conjure. "They all seemed to believe they were really speaking to their loved ones."

She decided not to mention Sharlyn's impersonation of Ben. If she accused Daniel of being in cahoots with the medium for some unknown reason, it would only cause Paige more concern. Plus, she was unsure as to whether what she'd experienced tonight was really a gift, as Daniel put it, or something not to be dallied with. Her nerves continued to ripple beneath her skin. Although Miss Dark had tugged her earlobe the same way Ben always did, her voice hadn't sounded anything like his. A good night's sleep would most likely help put the evening into perspective.

"Has Daniel ever mentioned that Miss Dark is blind?" she asked.

Paige was shocked. "No. Never. Is she?"

"I think so."

"You think? You're not sure?"

Briony remembered the way the beautiful woman had stared into her eyes as if she could see deep into her soul. She answered Paige's question with a question. "What purpose would she have for faking blindness?"

Paige shrugged. "Sounds like a night you'll never forget. You must be exhausted. I'm sorry I forced you to go."

"It's all right, but I am ready for bed. Getting up early this morning and traveling has caught up with me."

"Let me show you to your room. Mark moved your luggage upstairs already."

"That was nice of him." Briony wrapped her arm around Paige's waist and they started up the steps side-by-side. When they reached the guest room, Paige whispered, "I nearly forgot."

She gently shoved Briony into the room and then closed the door behind them. "I don't want to wake Mark and the baby." Her face broke into a wide smile. "Your detective phoned here tonight. He'd called your house, and your mother gave him my number. I took a message." She withdrew a slip of paper from the pocket of her dress and handed it to Briony.

Blood surged through her veins like a speeding train. "John called here?" She could hardly believe it. After three weeks of worrying and wondering if he was sick, dead, or simply not interested anymore, he'd gone to the trouble of tracking her down! That meant the world and more.

Paige had taken the message, so she'd heard his voice and knew what he'd said. She stood before her friend grinning like a satisfied cat that had licked up a full bowl of warm milk.

Briony opened the paper and skimmed the note. "John profusely apologizes for not having phoned before now, but he's had laryngitis!" She chuckled, and a sense of relief swelled her breast to know he wasn't hurt and he still cared about her. Her jaw dropped open when she read the next line. "He's taking time off and is planning a visit!"

"It's about time," Paige said. "You've been far more patient than I would have been."

"It's been the longest three months. He wants me to call him tomorrow to confirm that I still want him to come, and then he'll make arrangements." She pressed the paper to her chest and forced a rising squeal back down her throat. Paige wouldn't be pleased if she woke the baby.

"I take it you still want him to visit."

"You bet. He's all I've been thinking about since I came home from Maine."

"I'm happy for you," Paige said. "I can't wait for you to speak to him tomorrow." She hugged Briony.

"I'll let you get to bed now so you can dream about John. Thank you again for going with Daniel tonight. Good night. Hope you sleep well."

"I have a feeling I won't sleep at all now." She smiled. "Good night." She closed the door and stared at the note in her hand. Picturing John's rugged face, her body heated like a flame at the remembrance of the kisses they'd shared. Her skin prickled with excitement. He was coming to see her!

~ * ~

The next morning, she woke to rapping on the bedroom door. "Come in." She rose onto her elbows and rubbed her knuckles over her eyes.

The door opened. Paige's face was twisted into a frantic mask. "Amanda's running a high fever and cool rags aren't helping. Mark's left for work already. I'm driving her to the pediatrician's office."

Briony shot up straighter in the bed. "Oh, my. Shall I go with you?"

"No. I've got her bundled up and I'm ready to leave now. But thanks."

"Is there anything I can do in the meantime?"

"Actually, there is. Mark had planned on taking the day off, but he was called in to work for a mandatory meeting this morning. He and Daniel were scheduled to go pick up chairs from the rental store for the reception after the christening on Sunday. Would you mind going with Daniel to lend a hand?" Her face pinched. "I do hate to ask you. Hauling and lifting chairs isn't women's work."

"Don't be silly, Paige. When my father left us,

Mom and I often found ourselves helping Ben with chores that most people would consider men's work. I brought casual clothes with me. I'm glad to help."

Paige blew her a kiss. "You're a doll. Daniel's downstairs reading the paper over coffee. I've laid out some sweet rolls and fruit on the table. I was planning on fixing you a big breakfast of eggs and bacon and—"

Briony cut her off. "Don't worry yourself, Paige. I don't need you to baby me. I rarely eat breakfast anyway. Go on and take care of Amanda. Daniel and I will get the chairs. Is there anything else you need us to do while we're out?"

"I believe that's it for today. I'm not thinking clearly right now."

"I understand."

"Oh, there is one other thing I meant to tell you last night. Feel free to use the phone to call John whenever you want. It's located in the hallway next to the coat closet."

"Thank you. I'll be sure and pay you for the long distance call before I leave."

Paige shook her head. "I won't hear of it."

Amanda's soft cry drifted up the stairs. Paige cinched the belt of her wool coat and turned. "I need to go. Thank you!"

Briony called to her back. "You're welcome. Try not to worry. I'm sure Amanda's going to be fine."

Moments later, she heard Daniel assisting Paige out the front door. When the door closed, the house fell into silence. She felt slightly uncomfortable knowing it was only the two of them in the house. But they'd leave soon to go to the rental store, and Paige would probably be home by the time they returned with the chairs.

A peek out the window revealed a sunny morning. After a quick shower, she pulled her hair into a ponytail and changed into cigarette pants and a button-down cardigan. Downstairs, she greeted Daniel, who rose from the chrome kitchen table the moment she entered the room. He looked fresh and dapper in chinos and a pullover sweater.

"I trust you slept well." He folded the newspaper and refilled his mug with coffee.

"Yes, I did. The bed felt like a cloud. And you?"

He momentarily ignored her question. "Coffee?"

"Yes, please."

He poured a cup and handed it to her and retook his seat. "Sleep never comes easy to me. I haven't had one completely restful night in four months."

"I'm sorry. I hope you don't mind, but Paige told me about your fiancé, Monica. What a terrible tragedy. I understand she's the reason you visit Dark Hall."

A cloud passed across Daniel's face. "She is." His poignant eyes probed her. "You probably think I'm ridiculous for participating in séances."

"No, I don't." She sipped the coffee and plucked a sweet roll from the platter on the table. "I apologize for making you leave last night before Miss Dark was able to…"

"To summon Monica?" he finished. "It's all right. She's coming forth less and less. Sharlyn has told me spirits stop making their presence known when they feel they've accomplished what they set out to do."

Briony bit into the sweet roll. "Tell me what you mean."

"The last time Monica spoke through Sharlyn, she said she didn't want me to live my life alone. She asked me to remember her fondly, and she made me promise to move on and find someone new to love. That night, I had a feeling it was the final time we'd communicate, and it seems to have been. I've made peace with her passing and vowed to do as she requests. In fact, I believe I'm finally ready to start a new relationship." A shy smile parted his lips.

Paige was right. People did open up and confess their secrets to strangers. Briony thought about his comment. Was Daniel admitting he'd already moved on and had found someone else? Was that person Sharlyn Dark? Is that why he visited Dark Hall so many times a week? She'd seen the way he stared at the young woman last night, with more than admiration in his gaze. She believed he was in love with her.

Did Miss Dark share his passion? Had she planted the notion in his head about starting a new relationship by scripting Monica's final words to him? Briony wondered if that was somehow part of her scheme. Why would Miss Dark want to play Daniel? What did she see in him? He was a pleasant enough man with above average looks. But, of course, she was blind. Looks meant nothing to her. From what Briony gathered, Daniel didn't have much money either. But then, Miss Dark was the heiress to a fortune. She needed no money. Was she simply a lonely woman drawn to a lonely man?

She shrugged. Perhaps it was a love match after all and there was nothing for Paige and Mark to worry about. Anyway, it wasn't her business. "I understand we're to pick up some chairs for the reception on Sunday," she said, changing the subject.

Daniel stood up and placed his dirty dishes in the sink. "I can handle it alone. You're here on vacation. I'd never think of asking you to help."

"That's gallant of you, but I'm happy to. I don't want to sit in the house doing nothing. It looks like a beautiful morning. I'd like to see more of the city. That is, if you don't mind my tagging along."

He conceded it would be rude for him to leave her alone. She thought about her call to John, but Daniel appeared ready to go, so she decided not to keep him waiting. She could telephone John when they returned. She quickly finished her sweet roll and coffee, and the two of them headed out the door.

~ * ~

She didn't lift as much as a finger at the rental store. A young male employee helped Daniel carry the foldout chairs to the car and load them in the trunk. Briony stood watching while savoring the rays of the winter sun on her face.

"Why don't I give you a tour of the city since we're out?" Daniel suggested after slamming the trunk lid.

"I'd like that. I didn't see much of it yesterday with the rain falling."

He drove along the banks of Lake Michigan and past Lincoln Park Zoo. Then he pointed out the Union Railroad Station and stopped at the Buckingham Fountain where they got a closer look of its four pairs of bronzed seahorses. When they drove by the Science and Industry Museum, she gasped at the beauty of the building that was constructed of marble and limestone.

"Do you like museums?" he asked.

"Yes. I've read about this one. It's supposed to have three levels and more than 800 exhibits."

"I haven't been inside yet. Maybe before you leave, we could see the exhibits together."

She smiled; certain he wasn't flirting but was only being polite. "Perhaps Paige would like to come with us, too."

"She might, if getting ready for the christening hasn't worn her out."

Downtown, Daniel showed her the Chicago River and then drove by the white terracotta Wrigley building, the Chicago Board of Trade building, and the two magnificent towers that comprised the fairly new Lake Shore Drive apartment buildings whose exteriors were made of glass and steel.

After yesterday's rain and the strange evening spent at Dark Hall last night, Briony enjoyed the outing. A companionable alliance quickly formed between her and Daniel. Any awkwardness they'd experienced after the séance and on the drive home appeared to be gone. He seemed to be in his element as host and tour guide, and she was in an especially good mood. She eagerly anticipated talking to John later and felt like a flower that had bloomed out of the frozen ground.

"This certainly is a bustling city," she said as Daniel stopped the car at a red light downtown.

"Wichita is a good size town, isn't it?"

"Yes, but it doesn't hold a candle to Chicago. There's so much going on here." She rolled down the passenger window and a light breeze touched her face. People moved down the sidewalks in waves and came and went from shops like bees in and out of a hive. It was a work day, after all.

While waiting for the light to change, Daniel lowered his head and searched his pants pockets. "I must have a stick of gum in here somewhere," he mumbled. "I'm trying to quit smoking."

The signal flashed for pedestrians to cross the street. Briony glanced out the windshield and watched the stream of people as they passed by. When a familiar looking woman with long strawberry blonde hair walked in front of Daniel's car, she shook his arm.

"That looks like Miss Dark."

His head jerked up. As if she could hear their conversation, the woman stopped in the street. Her head turned. Ice blue eyes gazed directly at them.

A shudder ran through Briony. "It's her, isn't it?"

Daniel's jaw dropped.

The woman turned away quickly and fell back into the throng of people.

He frantically rolled his window down and shouted, "Sharlyn!"

"We have to be mistaken," Briony said, staring at the woman's retreating back. "Miss Dark is blind. Isn't she?"

Daniel didn't answer. The moment the light turned green, he pressed on the gas pedal and made a fast left.

CHAPTER FOUR

"There she is," he said, spotting the woman. She walked at a clipped pace across a public parking lot toward a blue and white Ford Fairlane convertible. Being winter, its top was up. He whipped his Coronet into the lot. The tires squealed in the gravel as he pulled beside her.

"Sharlyn!" He jumped out of the car and jogged around the front. The woman turned and stared blankly. With a flirtatious hand, she flipped a strand of shining hair over one shoulder.

From the car, Briony watched with rapt curiosity.

"Sharlyn," Daniel repeated. Stopping in front of her, he searched her face. Then his inquisitive gaze dipped to her body and raked her head to toe.

She cut a stunning figure dressed in a white belted trench coat that fell past her knees and was accented with a wide fur collar. Her high heels were red, as was her brimmed tilt hat that was trimmed with white satin and feathers. Her gaze seductively moved up and down Daniel's frame. A sly smile creased her mouth. Suddenly, the beaming light in her kindled eyes moved to Briony. Then her spirited gaze fell upon Daniel again, and she let out a sharp laugh.

What kind of game was she playing? A frown appeared between his eyebrows. With fists clenched at his sides, his expression was that of a man who realized he'd somehow been duped. Feeling pity for Daniel, Briony's temper sparked.

The low, rich sound of Miss Dark's voice cut through the air. "You have me mixed up with my sister. It happens all the time." She thrust her hand out to shake. "I'm Shelby Dark. And you are?" Her perfectly coiffed eyebrow arched.

Tentatively, he offered his hand. "Daniel Collier." A gentle rush of air expelled from his mouth, and the crease in his forehead vanished. "Your name is Shelby?" Chuckling nervously, a hand slid through his hair. "Wow. This makes better sense now. For a moment, I thought I'd lost my mind. Pleased to meet you." His lips formed a slow and wary smile. "I didn't know Sharlyn had a sister. She hasn't mentioned you."

Shelby rolled her eyes. "That comes as no surprise. Sharlyn pretends I don't exist. You see I'm the black sheep of the family. The *wild* one who doesn't play by the rules." She playfully slapped his arm. Her cool blue eyes sparkled with mischief and good humor, and another laugh filled the air.

Briony noticed the abrupt change in Daniel's demeanor. His spine grew straighter. His chin jutted forward. His cheeks warmed to a pleasant pink. Like a moth drawn to a bright flame, it seemed as if he'd instantly become smitten.

"You and Sharlyn look identical," he said.

"That's because we're identical twins, you silly man."

"Oh." His smile was a little too broad. "I had no idea she had family."

"Where do you know my sister from?" Shelby asked.

Daniel cleared his throat. "I was invited to Dark Hall by a friend several weeks ago. That's when we met."

Shelby narrowed her eyes. "Don't tell me you believe in that hocus pocus and voodoo she dishes out, Mr. Collier."

"Well…hmmm… I wouldn't exactly call what your sister does voodoo. She gives comfort to people in pain."

Shelby waved her hand as if it didn't matter. "If you believe Sharlyn can speak to the dead, then you must also think a one-legged man capable of kicking your ass in a fight." She crowed at her joke.

Briony felt her own cheeks warm. None of the women she knew would ever swear in public, especially in front of mixed company.

Like a snake seeking out its prey, Shelby flicked her full attention toward Briony. "Who have we here, Mr. Collier? Your girlfriend?" She strolled to the car and held her hand out.

Not wishing to be impolite, Briony clasped her hand through the open window. "We're not dating, Miss Dark. I'm Briony Martin, a friend of Mr. Collier's sister-in-law."

"How nice. *So* pleased to meet you." Thick eyelashes batting, Shelby's almond-shaped eyes delved into her. She held onto Briony's hand a bit longer than was comfortable, even squeezing it slightly. When she finally released it, she swung around and sashayed to her car. She stopped, as if she were thinking of something. Spinning quickly on her heel, her gaze fused with Briony's again. "Why don't we all have drinks together? Are you both free tonight?"

Daniel's face lit up. "I'm free."

Shelby stared so intently as to read Briony's most intimate thoughts. "And you, Miss Martin? Are you free as well?"

The woman's teasing and direct gaze were unnerving. Briony felt her face burn with mortification. Shelby Dark was flirting with her! And Daniel didn't even seem to notice. He stood there gawking at the woman like a lovesick puppy.

She swallowed past the tightness in her throat. "I'm spending the evening with my friend and her family. But thank you for the invitation," she added to be courteous.

"That's too bad," Shelby replied. She returned her bored gaze to Daniel. "Looks like it'll be just you and me, Mr. Collier. Seven o'clock tonight. My place." She rattled off the address. "Can you remember that?"

"Yes. I know the neighborhood. I'll be there." A stupid grin plastered his face.

"Ta-ta." She slid onto the leather seat of her convertible, gunned the motor, and left the parking lot in a swirl of dust.

Daniel climbed into his vehicle, moving like he had music in his bones. Briony had been so sure he was in love with Sharlyn. But it seemed all thoughts of the princess-like medium had been erased within moments. Her flamboyant twin with the firecracker attitude had captured his unbridled interest. Briony recalled the way Shelby had looked at her and shivered. She hoped Daniel hadn't made a mistake in agreeing to meet her for drinks. She had a feeling the woman's claws were sharper than a tiger's.

~ * ~

Upon returning home, Daniel began unloading the chairs from the trunk of his car into the shed in the back yard. Paige still wasn't home, so Briony decided to take advantage of a few moments of privacy and call John.

With a racing pulse, she sat at the telephone table in the hallway and dialed his number. The sound of the ring sounded far away in her ear. One, two, three, four jingles. No answer. She hung up and expelled a disappointed breath. He was probably out on a job.

She'd gotten halfway up the stairs when the telephone blared. Daniel was still outside, so she dashed down the steps and into the hall and grabbed the receiver.

"Hello, Collier residence."

After a brief pause, a deep voice said, "Briony? Is it you?"

Her heart ricocheted in her chest. "Yes, John! It's me. I just tried to call."

"I was unlocking the door and stepping through when I heard the phone ring. I couldn't reach it fast enough. I took a chance calling your friend's number, thinking it might have been you."

Unexpected tears sprang into her eyes. "It's so good to hear your voice, John. I thought something terrible had happened. Paige gave me your message last night, and I was relieved to know it was only laryngitis."

"I'm sorry to have worried you. I should have asked someone to phone and explain. But then, I couldn't talk, so that would have been hard to do." A deep chuckle rumbled up from his belly.

Briony smiled. "It's all right." Her heart twisted with longing, picturing his face. "Your message said you've got some free time coming up, and you plan to visit Kansas."

"If you still want me to." His voice teased.

Sparks flew through the telephone line to light a fire between them. "Of course I do! I've been waiting three months to see you again. I was afraid you'd changed your mind."

"Not a chance. I've been a fool to have not made time before now. But as I explained in our phone conversations, work piled up when you left Maine and I couldn't get away. I'm not letting anything stop me now. Would next weekend be too soon?"

"Next weekend?" Valentine's day was next Saturday. "No! It's not too soon. Will you fly or take the train?"

"I'll fly. I've already checked the airlines and schedules."

"You have?" Briony felt her heart would burst from her chest. "Oh, John, this is wonderful news. I can't wait for you to meet my mom and for me to show you around Wichita."

"I'm looking forward to both. But more than that, I'm anxious to spend time with you again. I don't care if we sit and stare at each other all day." His voice thickened with emotion. "I can't wait to hold you in my arms and kiss you. Every night I dream of the kisses we shared on Cape Marble."

A thrill raced up her spine and tingled the nape of her neck. "I do, too," she softly replied.

Aware that the long-distance minutes were ticking

by, she decided not to rack up the cost by explaining what had happened at Dark Hall last night. Aside from some peculiarities, there didn't seem to be any illegal activities going on there, as far as she could tell. Anyway, she wasn't going back, and Daniel was a grown man capable of making his own decisions, right or wrong. There was no advice she needed from John.

They said goodbye with him promising to call upon her return to Wichita Monday evening.

When the front door opened, she heard a muffled whimper. Paige had returned with Amanda. Daniel entered from the back door simultaneously and stepped into the living room.

"How's the baby?" Briony asked, moving forward to close the door and take Paige's purse and diaper bag from her shoulder.

Paige sat the straw basket on the couch and removed the blanket from over Amanda's head. "The doctor says there's nothing to worry about. The fever has already gone down. I guess it was a false alarm. I panicked for no reason." She smiled and kissed her baby's forehead.

"I'm sure your doctor has seen new mothers concerned over far less," Briony said. "Anyway, I've heard fever in a newborn is nothing to take lightly."

"You did the right thing," Daniel assured.

"Thanks, both of you. If you'll excuse me, Amanda's hungry. I'll give her a bottle and then put her in her crib."

After she'd gone upstairs, Daniel told Briony he'd unloaded all the chairs.

Knowing she should stay out of his business, she nonetheless felt compelled to warn him of the uneasiness that edged at her with regard to his date with Shelby Dark. "Are you sure you want to get involved with Shelby?" she blurted. "There's something about that woman that troubles me. Besides, I thought you liked her sister."

Daniel snorted. "You're quite observant, Briony. I have taken a fancy to Sharlyn. I like her very much, but it's not like we're spoken for each other. We've spent some time alone at the mansion, but we haven't even gone on a proper date outside of its gates. I don't see how it'll hurt to meet her twin for one drink. I might be able to garner information about Sharlyn from Shelby. Sharlyn's a mysterious girl. She doesn't talk about herself, and I want to know everything about her. She's beautiful and has a heart of gold."

Gathering information sounded like a good excuse. "But you're also attracted to Shelby," Briony pointed out. "And I suspect it has more to do with her behavior than her heart. I saw the way you stared at her."

He smiled. "You don't miss anything, do you, Briony? You caught me. The two women seem to be polar opposites, but I like them both in different ways."

She understood the way in which Daniel meant. It was pure physical attraction and Shelby's sassy attitude that enticed him. "They don't seem to be close. Shelby admitted as much. I doubt you'll get much information out of her about her sister. Her behavior bothered me. Didn't you think she acted strangely?"

"Strange? In what way?"

Was he kidding? How was it possible for him not

to have noticed the blatant way in which Shelby had flirted with her? Briony wrung her hands together and remembered the story her mother had once told her in passing about a great aunt who had lived with another woman for forty years. At the great aunt's funeral, the other woman had caused a scene by throwing herself upon the casket and sobbing for the loss of *her dearest and sweetest love*. The next day, she'd been arrested on suspicion of participating in a *demented* relationship. That was in the 1930s. As it turned out, she'd been able to hire a good lawyer and was able to avoid jail time. However, the poor woman had been run out of town on a rail, so the story went. No one in the family ever learned what had happened to her.

Briony wondered if Shelby Dark preferred women over men in the same way Mother's great aunt had. If so, why ask Daniel over for a drink? He excused himself and disappeared into his room to leave her alone with the question unanswered.

~ * ~

Around eight o'clock that evening, Briony, Paige and Mark were enjoying lively conversation in the living room when the back door slammed open. Daniel stumbled into the room looking as white as a sheet. Mark bounded up from the couch.

"What's wrong, man? You look as if you've seen a ghost."

Daniel leaned against the wall, as if he might pass out. Mark rushed to him and grabbed his arm. Their hands touched, and when Mark slipped out of Daniel's grasp, his palms were stained red.

"Good Lord, Daniel! Is that blood?"

The women jumped from their seats. Paige uttered a sharp cry. A cold chill washed over Briony when her gaze met Daniel's. Grave lips and a troubled brow indicated something wicked had occurred at Shelby Dark's tonight.

"Where have you been? What happened? Were you in an accident?" Mark demanded answers. He led Daniel to a cushioned chair and pushed down on his shoulder to lower him into the seat. Then Mark knelt on a knee in front of his brother.

"I'll wet a wash cloth to clean his hands," Paige said, running to the bathroom.

Briony stood at Daniel's side. "Did something happen at Shelby's house?" she asked.

A frightened expression glazed his eyes. He nodded.

"Who's Shelby?" Mark asked.

"Sharlyn Dark's twin sister." She quickly explained how they'd met her today, and how she'd invited Daniel for a drink.

"Whose blood is on your hands, Daniel?" Mark asked.

Paige returned with the cloth. Daniel was in such a bewildered state, he didn't move, so she wiped his hands. "We should phone the police. Shouldn't we?" she asked Mark.

"Not yet." Briony lowered to her knees and gazed into Daniel's eyes. "Tell us what happened. Don't leave any detail out."

He took a few moments to compose himself and then began. "I arrived at the address Shelby had given me promptly at seven o'clock. The building was a brownstone downtown. I rang the doorbell and waited, but no one answered. I rang again. Still, no one came to the door. Feeling like I was being watched, I turned my head and saw someone next door duck quickly into the shadows. I guessed it was a nosy neighbor. Instead of ringing the bell a third time, I lifted the brass knocker on the door. That's when I realized the door was ajar. I pushed it further open and called out hello. The foyer was dark. I stuck my head in a bit and could see there were no lights on inside, which I found odd, since Shelby was expecting me at seven. I called out her name. Still no response." He paused and inhaled a deep breath through his nose.

"Go on," Briony urged. "What did you do next?"

"A sense of dread and foreboding suddenly came over me. The air inside the brownstone was thick and stale, like the house had been closed up for a long time, and it smelled of something sweet. And then I heard it."

"It?"

"A moan. It was the sound of a human, not an animal. Someone inside was hurt or sick. At least, that's what I imagined. Naturally, I thought it was Shelby, so I barged through the door and followed the noise to the parlor. The room was deep in shadows, but I could see the shape of a body lying on the floor, face up."

Paige covered her mouth with her hand.

"I rushed forward and had just bent to see that the person lying on the floor wasn't Shelby at all, but a man, when I heard footsteps rush behind me. Before I could turn, I was hit in the head and rendered unconscious." He touched his scalp and fresh blood coated his fingers.

"Good God!" Mark exclaimed.

Briony rose and gently examined the gash in the back of his skull. "The injury is deep. It's going to need stitches."

"It'll wait," Daniel said. "I want to finish my story. When I woke up, I had a God-awful headache and remembered being bashed with something. But what I was most concerned about was the body next to me."

"Did you touch it?" Briony asked. "To check for a pulse?"

"No. The poor fellow was obviously dead. He wasn't breathing, and there was dried blood on his mouth. Then I saw the hole in his shirt and more blood around the wound. He'd been shot. I panicked. There was no way to know if whoever had killed him and clocked me in the head was still in the house, so I gathered my wits and ran. I should have called the police, but I was afraid they'd think I was the perpetrator."

"And you have no idea if Shelby was in the house?" Briony asked.

He shook his head. "For all I know, someone murdered her, too. I should have searched the house." He hung his head in his hands. "I didn't know what to do. I wasn't thinking clearly."

Mark patted his leg. He clenched his teeth and flashed a fearful look at Paige and Briony. "What do we do now?"

"We have to get him to the hospital," Paige said. "Besides stitching that wound, he might have a concussion."

"First, Daniel must call the police," Briony said.

His head lifted. "No! The neighbor next door will tell them she saw me at Shelby's door, and they'll accuse *me* of the murder."

Briony's voice remained calm. "Not if you didn't have a motive. Maybe the man committed suicide. Did you see a gun near the body?"

He thought a minute. "No."

"No murder weapon found at the scene means your prints won't be found on it either," she reasoned logically. "From what you told us, your fingerprints will only be found on the doorknob and doorbell, and the knocker. That proves nothing except that you were at the house, and you were there by invitation of the owner. When you realized the door was open and you heard a noise inside, you went to investigate, thinking Shelby was injured or sick. The police will have no reason to suspect you of wrongdoing, especially if you have no connection to the victim."

"You must have learned a thing or two from your boyfriend," Paige said. "You're thinking just like a private eye."

"I hear a lot of testimony from cops in my job." She smiled, proud of the clarity in which she perceived this situation. "Don't you see, Daniel, you have to tell the police your side of the story? If you don't and they discover you were there tonight, they'll definitely think you have something to hide and you may end up a suspect despite the lack of physical evidence. Besides, don't you want to know if Shelby is all right?"

"Of course I do."

"Then the police need to be notified immediately

so they can go search her brownstone for her and for clues."

"What if they find her dead, too?"

An icy feeling slid up her arms. "What if they don't? To me, that's the more important question."

Daniel's head tilted. A flash of comprehension lit in his eyes. "Do you think she might have killed the man? Do you think she set me up?"

"I don't know the woman," Mark spoke up, "but if the police find no sign of forced entry, the victim was obviously let in by someone. Being the owner of the brownstone, this Shelby Dark person seems the likeliest suspect in his death."

Paige worried her lip between her teeth. "Why did whoever shot the man have to hit Daniel in the head?"

"The crime had probably just been committed," Mark stated. "Obviously, the killer was still in the house when Daniel arrived. He or she couldn't leave behind a witness." A muscle quivered in his jaw, and he squeezed his brother's arm. "We're lucky you have a hard head." They shared weak smiles. "I agree with Briony," he continued. "You need to phone the police. Then I'll drive you to the emergency room."

Daniel was a lucky man indeed, Briony thought. Something hinted a malevolent force had been at work tonight. She didn't believe for a moment that he'd coincidentally walked in on a murder.

CHAPTER FIVE

Mid-day the following morning, Mark and Daniel sat at the kitchen table with Briony and Paige rehashing the events as they happened last night. After a visit to the emergency room where Daniel received ten stitches in his scalp, Mark had driven him to Chicago Police Department headquarters to give his statement. There, they learned the next-door neighbor had called the police after hearing a gunshot from inside Shelby's brownstone.

A Sergeant Montague informed them that the victim's name was Andrew Whealdon. "Do you know him?" the sergeant asked.

Daniel did not.

"Are you certain? Perhaps you and Mr. Whealdon were both involved with Miss Dark, found yourselves at her apartment at the same time, argued over her, and an argument got out of hand."

"I don't know the victim," Daniel maintained. "I don't even know Miss Dark, to be honest. I just met her today for the first time. Miss Martin will attest to that."

The sergeant telephoned Briony at the Collier home, and she verified Daniel's statement. After another forty minutes of questioning, Montague admitted there was no physical evidence linking Daniel to the crime, so he wasn't placed under arrest.

Since he wasn't entirely cleared of suspicion, however, the sergeant asked him to be available in case there was need to question him further.

The sergeant also told Daniel and Mark that Shelby Dark had not been found in the brownstone. There had been no forced entry and nothing seemed to have been stolen. No furniture was out of place, which indicated there'd been no struggle. As of late last night, there had been no sign of her.

"I want to go to Dark Hall and speak to Sharlyn," Daniel now said, rising from his chair. "Maybe Shelby is there, or Sharlyn's heard from her."

"I don't think that's a good idea," Mark replied. "Let the cops handle this. The more distance you put between you and those two crazy women, the better, in my opinion."

From the twist of his mouth, it was clear Daniel took offense to his brother's statement. "Sharlyn's not crazy. She's a good person. If she doesn't know her sister's missing, I owe it to her to let her know."

"I don't see why you owe that witch anything," Paige chimed in. "Mark and I knew she was trouble from the first time you met her, and apparently, her twin is worse than trouble. She may be a killer."

"That's not fair. You don't know anything of the sort. Maybe Shelby was defending herself from an intruder. Anyway, it doesn't matter what either of you think. I'm going to see Sharlyn." Daniel stood up and wobbled a bit. His eyes squinted closed, and he winced. It was evident his head still hurt.

"If you're determined to go," Briony said, "I'll go with you. You shouldn't be driving."

His face broadened into a grateful smile. "I'd

appreciate that, Briony. At least you understand. I can't sit around here doing nothing and wondering what's happened to Shelby."

"Maybe her sister the medium can summon her," Mark said smugly, rising to refill his coffee cup.

"Only if she's dead," Mark answered between tight lips. "Let's hope that's not the case. Let's go, Briony." He retrieved his car keys from the pocket of his jacket hanging on the peg and tossed them to her. Then he exited the kitchen door, slamming it behind him.

"I shouldn't have said that." Mark shook his head. "I don't wish anyone dead."

"And I shouldn't have called that woman a witch," Paige mumbled.

"It's been a long and stressful night for all of us," Briony replied. "Paige, do you need any help this morning? I should have asked you before offering to go with Daniel."

"No worries. Mark had already requested the day off to help with final preparations. I'm glad you're going with Daniel. You'll be able to stay objective when he speaks to Miss Dark. Perhaps you'll be able to use your newly acquired detective skills and pick up on something that will be helpful to the police."

"I'll try. See you both later."

~ * ~

After Daniel announced their names over the intercom, the sour-faced butler opened the door and escorted them inside Dark Hall. "Wait here." He disappeared into a room to the right of the foyer.

"That's the library," Daniel whispered.

A moment later, the butler stepped out of the room and approached. "Miss Dark will see you." Keeping pace with his long-legged gait, they followed him across the foyer and entered the library. All four walls were filled with floor to ceiling bookcases stacked with hardbound books. The ceiling was painted with frescos portraying scenes from the Renaissance era, and full-sized marble statues of nude men and women were stationed around the room. A fire crackled in a large stone hearth. The butler bowed and closed the door behind them.

A brilliant smile lit Sharlyn's pale face when she heard their footfalls cross the wooden floor. She perched on the edge of a settee that was covered in a rich shade of midnight blue suede. An open book was cradled in her palms, which Briony thought odd since she was blind. Her assistant, Lee, sat stiffly beside her dressed in slacks and a man's button down shirt and bow tie. The aura she emitted was one of suspicion and protection, like a bulldog shielding its owner.

"Daniel! How wonderful of you to visit. And I understand you've brought your friend, Miss Martin, with you as well," Sharlyn said.

"Hello, Sharlyn." He cupped her small hand in his and held it a moment.

"Thank you for seeing us on the spur of the moment," Briony said.

Miss Dark's bright eyes fused with hers. Like the night they met, her gaze delved deep. Briony's pulse skipped a beat. The few blind people she'd come into contact with wore sunglasses or they squinted and moved their head around as they spoke. In some cases, their pupils rolled upward in their sockets. Not so with Sharlyn. The ocean blue depths of her eyes were as clear as glass, and her steady gaze held Briony in an iron grip. Most likely, Miss Dark had become blind later in life, as opposed to being born without sight. Even so, her direct gaze was unsettling.

"Please have a seat," she said, indicating with a wave of her hand the two club chairs positioned across from the settee. Her strawberry blonde hair was fashioned into one side braid and tied with a ribbon at the end. Elegant in a forest green skirt and white cashmere sweater, she was not at all the woman Paige feared was some kind of witch.

Her pink lips lifted into a smile, and her voice teased. "I know you're watching me, Miss Martin."

Briony's shoulders grew rigid as steel. "How rude of me. I'm sorry."

Sharlyn chuckled. "Don't be. It's natural to be curious as to how a handicapped person functions in daily life. It's not as bad as you might imagine. When someone has lost one of her senses, all the others become heightened to an almost extrasensory degree. I suppose it's God's way of overcompensating for the loss."

"That makes sense," Daniel said.

Sharlyn's head turned toward Lee. Her assistant hadn't uttered a word, not even a hello. Her tense frame spoke volumes.

"Say hello to our guests, Lee," Sharlyn said, sweetly.

"Hello."

Briony and Daniel exchanged a subtle glance. What was this relationship about? Briony wondered.

"What do I owe the pleasure of your visit?" Sharlyn asked. She flipped the book on her lap closed and placed it on a tea table beside the settee.

Daniel spoke up. "I'm afraid we have some—"

"What were you reading?" Briony interrupted. She tossed a knowing glance at him, hoping he'd understand why she'd cut him off. Suddenly, she felt it very important to learn more about the relationship between the two women before her.

"We were reading one of my favorite poems, *The Raven*, by Edgar Allan Poe," answered Sharlyn. "Many of the classics have been translated into Braille."

"Nevermore, nevermore," Daniel crowed, causing Briony to jump. When no one laughed, the tips of his ears grew pink.

"Are you familiar with Poe, Miss Martin?" Sharlyn asked, ignoring Daniel's silly outburst.

"Please call me Briony. And I am, although he's not a favorite. Do you often read literature that focuses on the supernatural?"

"Because I'm a medium, do you mean? *The Raven* is often noted for its musicality and stylized language, Briony. Not only for its supernatural atmosphere. It also makes use of a number of folk and classical references."

"So I understand. Poe claimed to have written the poem logically and methodically, intending to create a piece that would appeal to both the critical and popular tastes of the time."

She nodded. "Its publication made the author widely popular, even if it didn't bring him much financial success."

"Nevertheless, it remains one of the most famous poems ever written."

Sharlyn clapped her hands like a child, evidently enjoying the banter. "I daresay you've studied Poe more than you'd led us to believe, Briony."

"I said he wasn't my favorite. I didn't say I hadn't thoroughly studied the poem. I know *The Raven's* theme is one of undying devotion. The narrator experiences a perverse conflict between the desire to forget and the desire to remember. He seems to get some pleasure from focusing on loss. Do you agree with my interpretation, Lee?" Her gaze shifted to the young woman pretending to be a man.

Lee's gaze snapped up, eyes widened. She looked to Sharlyn, as if requesting permission to speak.

"Go ahead. Answer the question," Sharlyn urged in a tender voice. "I like when you join in the conversation."

Lee cleared her throat. "The poem is prophetic."

"Oh? In what way?" Daniel asked.

Lee's gaze dropped to her lap. Silence alone could express the emotion of the moment.

Sharlyn's fingers found her hand. She squeezed it as if to bolster her courage. "Don't be afraid to voice your opinion, Lee. It's not often you and I find ourselves involved in a stimulating discussion regarding literature, is it?"

"No, it's not." Lee offered a shaky smile and drew a breath into her lungs before expounding on the subject she knew well. "When the raven steps into the narrator's chamber and the narrator asks his name, the raven's only answer is: nevermore. The narrator is surprised the bird can talk. Each question he asks the raven after that is responded with that one word: nevermore. As the narrator recalls his lost love, Lenore, to the raven, the air grows denser and he feels the presence of angels. He wonders if God is sending him a sign that he is to forget Lenore. When he asks the bird if he should forget Lenore, the raven again replies in the negative, suggesting that the narrator can never be free of his memories. The narrator then becomes angry, calling the raven a thing of evil and a prophet. He remarks to himself that his friend the raven will soon fly out of his life, just as other friends have flown before, along with his previous hopes. The narrator's final admission is that his soul is trapped beneath the raven's shadow and shall be lifted nevermore."

Lee paused.

"Why do you claim the poem to be prophetic?" Daniel asked.

Her voice lowered. "Some scholars suggest the poem is a type of Ancient Greek or Roman form consisting of the lament of an excluded lover at the sealed door of his beloved. In the end, the narrator becomes regretful and grief-stricken before passing into a frenzy and, finally, madness. In that way it is prophetic."

For what seemed an eternity, no one spoke. Briony wondered if the prophecy she addressed in her discourse was actually the narrator's in Poe's poem or that of the foretelling of her own life.

Sharlyn shook her head in disbelief. Perhaps she'd never heard Lee string so many words together at one time. When at last it seemed her shock had ebbed, she chuckled and patted Lee's thigh. "That's quite an intellectual analysis. I didn't know you knew so much about Poe and his work. Did you study him at Mount Carmel High?"

"Mount Carmel High?" Briony inquired.

"It's an all boys Catholic high school here in Chicago."

This was ridiculous! Briony quelled the urge to blurt out that she knew Lee was a woman, not a man. What was the point of their charade? She stared, contemplating. Lee's burning hot gaze seared two holes straight through her, suggesting a challenge.

Briony found Lee's speech to be more than an intellectual analysis. Something hinted a deep personal connection between her and the poem. But what exactly did it mean? Her gaze shifted between her and Sharlyn. The two women were obviously close and shared an interest in the supernatural, through literature and séances. Though interesting, Briony wasn't sure how, or if, the dots connected. And whether any of it made a difference. Maybe she was following a lead that wasn't a lead at all. Perhaps she'd have to call John again and ask for his advice, after all.

Daniel's voice broke into her thoughts. "This has been fascinating, but our purpose for coming today is not so pleasant, Sharlyn. I'm afraid we have some bad news."

"Oh?"

"It has to do with your sister, Shelby."

"Shelby? How on earth do you know about her?" The color seemed to drain from her angelic face.

In a nutshell, Daniel explained how he and Briony had met Shelby. Then he told her about the man named Andrew Whealdon who'd been found shot in

Shelby's brownstone, and how Shelby appears to be missing. He ended by showing her the back of his head. "Someone tried to kill me, too."

She uttered a sharp cry and seemed genuinely concerned. Oddly, she didn't ask why Daniel had gone to Shelby's brownstone in the first place.

"When we had our private talks, why didn't you mention your twin?" he asked her.

Briony may have imagined it, but she thought she saw Lee flinch.

"I saw no need," Sharlyn answered. Her hand fluttered at her chest. "My sister and I haven't seen each other in nearly six months. We're as different as day and night. We have nothing in common. I don't approve of her lifestyle. She abuses alcohol and drugs, and men, among other things."

If that statement surprised Daniel, he didn't let on.

"Apparently, she doesn't approve of yours, either," Briony said, remembering how Shelby had called Sharlyn's profession hocus pocus and voodoo.

"I gave up caring what my sister thought about me or anyone else a long time ago," Sharlyn replied. "She suffers from emotional problems. It's sad and I'm sorry to air our dirty laundry, but the truth is the truth."

Lee nodded her head, though ever so slightly as to not be observed by anyone but Briony's keen eye.

"Do you know this man, Andrew Whealdon?" Daniel asked.

Sharlyn's hesitation spoke for her.

"How do you know him?" he pressed.

She folded her hands in her lap. "He was Shelby's boyfriend. I suppose that's one way of describing him and their relationship. Frankly, they behaved more like dogs in heat when they were together. Disgusting. Andrew was one in a long line of men Shelby used and then disposed of when she tired of them."

Briony's ears perked. "Was? Did Shelby break up with him?"

"Yes. Andrew came by Dark Hall to cry on my shoulder. He said he couldn't live without her or some such nonsense. He begged me to talk to her."

"When was this?"

"Two weeks ago. I told him I had no idea where she was keeping herself. Besides, I'd tried to warn him before he got involved with her, but he didn't listen. None of them ever did. Shelby seems to cast a spell over men. They became putty in her hands."

Briony cast a glance at Daniel. He'd fallen under Shelby's hypnotic spell, too. Look how that had turned out. At least he wasn't dead, though it had been a close call.

She wondered if Andrew Whealdon *had* committed suicide when Shelby refused him once again. But if he had, where was the gun he'd used? Her mind spun with possible scenarios.

It seemed most likely that Shelby had answered the door thinking it was Daniel. Andrew had burst in and, when she wouldn't agree to get back together, he killed himself in front of her. Perhaps she'd panicked and touched the gun before realizing her fingerprints would be found on it. Someone might have heard the gunshot, she'd reason. So she knew she didn't have much time before police arrived. Maybe she'd taken the weapon to another part of the house to clean her fingerprints off. When she heard Daniel enter the brownstone and call out her name, she didn't know how she'd explain the situation. Without thinking, she crept up behind him and hit him on the head, not intending to seriously hurt him, and fled the brownstone with the gun. Now she was in hiding.

It made sense, in a way. But why not call the police herself and explain that Andrew had committed suicide in front of her? If his prints, and his alone, were found on a gun registered in his name, she wouldn't have been charged with any crime. Did she have something else to hide? Something she didn't want the police, or anyone else, to know?

"Shelby hasn't contacted you in the past fifteen or so hours?" Daniel asked Sharlyn.

"No. If she does, what should I do?"

"Convince her to tell you where she is. Or talk her into coming to Dark Hall. I suggest you contact the police department and tell them you're her sister. Show them you're willing to cooperate. Shelby may not have done anything wrong, but a man died in her house. They need to question her. If she's not guilty of a crime, she has nothing to fear."

"I understand. I take it you've been cleared of the crime?"

"I'm not high on their list of suspects anymore. I think the ten stitches in my head helped sway them."

She sighed. "Thank goodness. What a terrible ordeal you've been through. I appreciate your both coming by to fill me in." She abruptly stood and nodded to Lee, who indicated the visit was over.

"Miss Dark needs to rest now," she said. "She has a séance to prepare for tonight. Will you be attending, Mr. Collier?"

He shook his head. "Not tonight. My head still

hurts."

"Will I be hearing from you again soon?" Sharlyn asked him. "I've enjoyed the time we've spent alone recently. I do hope to see much more of you, privately." Her skirt swished when she moved forward and planted her hands on his arms. She smoothed her expression into a sweet mask and kissed both of his cheeks, European style.

His mild embarrassment was apparent, but from Briony's viewpoint, the nymph had enchanted him once again. "I'll be in touch soon," he promised.

Lee strode to a pull-cord near the door and yanked on it. Within moments, the butler appeared. Briony and Daniel said their goodbyes and trailed him to the front door.

Outside, she slid onto the driver's seat of the Coronet and started the car. He settled his weight into the passenger seat and heaved a great sigh. "Isn't she lovely?"

Without commenting, Briony pressed on the gas. She passed through the gate and glanced in the rearview mirror. Instead of looking smaller the further down the driveway she drove, the mansion appeared to expand into a living, breathing creature. A lump of fear crawled up her throat. Was Paige right? Was some kind of witchcraft being practiced there? Daniel behaved like a man under a spell. He seemed oblivious to the strange magnetic pull that had drawn him to both of the Dark women. Couldn't he feel what she did? That something sinister hid within the depths of Dark Hall?

She turned off of Lake Shore Drive and sped up the car, praying he'd never return to Dark Hall again.

If the spasms in her stomach meant something, Daniel could very well become its next victim.

CHAPTER SIX

Briony parked the car at the curb in front of the Collier home. When she and Daniel entered the house, Paige met them at the front door. Her face was stretched into a mask of terror. Trembling, her voice climbed an octave higher than usual.

"Thirty minutes ago, Sergeant Montague of the police department phoned. He wants to speak to you again, Daniel. He asked you to call this number." With a shaking hand, she passed him a slip of paper with a phone number on it. "He would like for you to meet him at the police station, but I suggest you ask the sergeant to come here instead."

"Why? What's happened? You look scared to death."

"I am. Something was pushed through the mail slot in the front door not ten minutes ago." She strode to the coffee table and picked up an envelope and thrust it at him. His name was typed on the front. After reading the letter inside, his eyes bulged. "Where's Mark? Has he seen this?"

"Yes. He's upstairs with the baby. She started crying right before you walked in. He's rocking her back to sleep."

"Did you or he see who put this through the slot?" Daniel asked.

She shook her head. "The mail comes in the

afternoon, so it wasn't the postman."

"There's no stamp or postmark," he noted.

"I was in the kitchen," Paige continued. "I heard the squealing of tires, and it sounded close, so I glanced out the window and saw the tail end of a car heading down the street. I didn't hear anyone approach the door. No one knocked or rang the bell. When I stepped into the living room, I saw the envelope on the foyer floor." She looked ready to burst into tears. "What does it mean, Daniel?"

Briony's curiosity could wait no longer. "May I see what the fuss is about?" She reached for the paper in his hand. Her gaze moved across the typed words that threatened Daniel with death if he didn't mind his own business and leave the Dark women alone. Realizing too late that she'd broken the most basic of investigatory rules, she gritted her teeth in frustration. "We've all touched both the envelope and the paper, which we shouldn't have done. Our fingerprints may have smudged those of the person who sent this."

Paige's mouth gaped. "I'm sorry. I didn't think…" Her lips quivered, and then her gaze shifted to Daniel. With eyes suddenly flashing, she ground out, "This is all happening because you got mixed up with Dark Hall. We've heard the rumors. I knew that place was evil. You almost got yourself killed. You still might! Now you've involved not only me and Mark, but also my best friend!"

Briony wrapped her arm around Paige. "Let's all stay calm. Daniel will call Sergeant Montague right now, and he'll come over and sort everything out. The police will know what to do. It'll be all right, you'll see." Daniel stood with a blank expression on his face.

Briony nudged him in the ribs. "Go call the policeman. Now."

~ * ~

Sergeant Montague donned plastic gloves. He read the note and then put it back into the envelope and slipped the envelope into a plastic bag as evidence. Next, he dusted the outside of the mail slot and front door for prints. When he'd finished, he lowered his weight onto the couch.

"It's unlikely we'll be able to lift fingerprints off the envelope and paper since all of you touched them." His mouth tightened with annoyance, and his gaze flitted around the room. "But if we're lucky, we might get a hit off the mail slot or door." He leaned toward the coffee table and grabbed the mug of coffee that Paige had offered him upon arrival. He took a sip. "In the meantime, Mr. Collier, I'd suggest lying low. A death threat is nothing to take lightly."

"You haven't found Shelby yet, I take it?" he asked.

"No. No sign of her or the murder weapon. We went through her brownstone with a fine-toothed comb. Funny, but it doesn't appear to be lived in."

"What do you mean?"

"It must not be her permanent residence. There's no homey feeling. It's sparsely furnished. You probably weren't there long enough to notice, but there are no photos anywhere in the house. The kitchen has no pots or pans in the cupboards. No food in the refrigerator. The liquor cabinet is stocked, however. And there are clothes hanging in the closet of the bedroom we assume to be hers."

"What type of clothes?" Briony asked.

"Dresses, shoes, hats, nylon stockings…female clothing."

"But what style?" she persisted. "Dressy, casual, expensive, plain?"

His gaze was direct. "A lot of the stuff looked like it belonged to a street walker, if you want my honest opinion."

Paige gasped. "Is that what she is, Daniel?"

"Of course not," he snapped. "Briony met her. She wasn't dressed anything like a…a…that type of woman."

Montague went on. "My people found makeup and perfume bottles and lipsticks on the vanity table. We also discovered cocaine hidden in her underwear drawer. If and when we find Shelby Dark, she'll be brought up on a narcotics charge."

Daniel paled.

"I knew it," Paige said, crossing her arms over her chest.

"You said it was the other one who was involved in drugs," Mark reminded her.

"The other one?" the sergeant said. "Do you mean Sharlyn Dark?"

"Yes," Briony answered. "I see you know about her."

"The neighbor who called in the gunshot told us there's a twin. The neighbor met her once. She said she came home from work one afternoon to find who she thought was Shelby sitting on her outside steps looking dazed and confused. Having thought she'd locked herself out of her apartment, the neighbor offered to call a locksmith. That's when she discovered it wasn't Shelby at all. The woman introduced herself as Shelby's twin, Sharlyn. The two engaged in pleasant conversation for a few moments. That's when the neighbor realized the woman was blind. Then Sharlyn suddenly excused herself, carefully made her way down the steps, and disappeared down the street."

Sitting next to Daniel on the loveseat, Briony sensed a distinct hum mushrooming from him. She felt it vibrate between them like a tuning fork.

The policeman continued. "Sharlyn Dark lives in a castle called Dark Hall on Lake Shore Drive. You've probably heard of the place. We interviewed her late last night. From what she told us, the sisters inherited the mansion from their grandfather, Oliver, when he died ten years ago. They were only thirteen years old at the time. They never knew their father. Their mother—Oliver's daughter—has lived in a mental institution since the girls were toddlers. Miss Dark told us their former housekeeper raised her and her sister."

"Did you know that about her family history?" Mark asked Daniel.

He shook his head, trying hard to hide his surprise. "She hasn't talked about her past."

"What was the housekeeper's name?" Briony inquired.

Montague checked his notes. "I don't have that written down and can't seem to recall at the moment." He jotted some notes into the pad on his thigh and then took another sip of coffee. "When I questioned Miss Dark about her grandfather's death, she said it had been an accident. He fell down the spiral staircase and died upon impact at the bottom of the steps. There was an accident report filed. Our department records corroborate her statement."

A vague unease snuck along Briony's chest wall. "Excuse me, Sergeant Montague. I wonder if you might be able to do more research into his death? Can you get access to the city's medical records? Is the coroner who conducted the autopsy on Oliver Dark still alive?"

He hitched his shoulders in a slight shrug and chuckled. "Who have we here? Nancy Drew?"

Smiling, she was pleased to be compared to one of her favorite fictional heroines. "I think it would be helpful to confirm that the grandfather's death *was* simply an accident, as the documentation claimed at the time."

"What are you getting at, Miss…?

"Miss Martin of Wichita, Kansas." She cleared her throat. "Being a family of extreme wealth, it's conceivable that the Dark sisters, or someone on their behalf used their power and influence to convince the coroner to list Oliver Dark's death as an accident on the certificate."

"There's no reason to believe it wasn't an accident. Do you know something I don't?"

"Call it a hunch," she said.

He shifted his weight and leaned forward, interest sparking his clear eyes. "The Chicago Police Department doesn't work on hunches, ma'am. Are you suggesting someone paid the coroner to forge a death certificate?"

"It's possible, is it not? Maybe the fall wasn't an accident at all. It might be worth doing a little digging into the past, considering the Dark women have found themselves at the center of a suspicious death."

The sergeant rolled his eyes. "Now you're telling me how to do my job, Miss Martin?"

Heat crept up her throat. "I'm sorry, Sergeant. I should keep my mouth shut."

He chuckled. "It's okay. Actually, that's a good idea. Doctor Crisman has been Chicago's coroner for twenty years. He's still alive and well. I'll have one of my men pop over and interview him immediately. I'll authorize them to bring him to headquarters if the good doctor proves to be uncooperative."

Daniel's head turned, and he glared at her. Irritation barely contained his body. No doubt, he felt a sting of betrayal. She was suggesting the woman he cared for might be involved shady dealings, even if he'd yet to admit his love for Sharlyn.

Montague added one final thought. "Last night, Miss Dark claimed she and her sister haven't been in touch for a long time."

"We spoke to her a couple of hours ago," Daniel said. "She didn't mention having talked to you last night. I'm sure she's worried and confused. It probably slipped her mind to tell us."

Briony struggled to tamp down anger that flared in the pit of her stomach. He was making excuses for Sharlyn. Why *hadn't* she mentioned the sergeant's visit? She'd acted surprised when Daniel told her about Shelby and Andrew Whealdon. That meant she'd lied to them, even if it was by omission. Probably, she was hiding her twin at Dark Hall, too. Having been a twin herself, Briony would have done anything for Ben. But she would have drawn the line at murder!

"*You* spoke to Sharlyn Dark? I don't understand." Montague's gaze narrowed.

"I'm acquainted with both sisters," Daniel confessed. "I met Sharlyn several weeks ago. I only met Shelby yesterday."

"Why didn't you mention this when I interviewed you last night?"

"I'm sorry. I wasn't thinking clearly, having been attacked and left with a concussion and wounded head. I was in a confused state myself."

"Ah, yes. I suppose that's understandable." Montague's expression didn't hold much sympathy. Policemen were used to criminals lying and covering up facts, and he probably didn't have much patience for people who didn't fully cooperate with them. His steady gaze raked over the others. "When I questioned Miss Dark about Andrew Whealdon, she said he's been a client of hers for a few months and that he met Shelby through her. Apparently, Miss Dark is a psychic or clairvoyant or some such, and she holds séances and claims to speak to the dead. She said Mr. Whealdon told her he'd lost both his parents and he came to her hoping to communicate with them."

Briony spoke up. "Wait a minute. You said he'd been her client for three months? That doesn't make sense. Sharlyn told us she hasn't seen or spoken to Shelby in close to six months."

"Is that so? She failed to mention that important fact. Seems to be a lot of that going around." The policeman frowned at Daniel and then scratched the new information into his notebook. "The victim was fairly new to Chicago. He came here eight months ago from Nebraska and was working for the Chicago Daily News. He was a rookie reporter and evidently anxious to move up the ladder quickly, according to his co-workers. My partner's at the precinct right now reading through all of Whealdon's articles to see if he wrote anything about Dark Hall."

Briony leaned forward, grasping his theory. "Do you think he might have pretended to be a client so he could get access to Dark Hall and write an investigative report about Sharlyn and what she does for a living?"

"That's one angle we're looking at. It's possible he was investigating her involvement in fraud—taking advantage of people financially—that sort of thing. One of my men turned up a couple of complaints from previous clients of Miss Dark's, which involved money. Whealdon's co-workers said he'd been working on a special project, but he kept hush-hush about it. The editor of the paper didn't have any idea of what he was up to. He hadn't given him an assignment involving Dark Hall. The co-workers only knew there was something Whealdon was anxious to shed light upon, and he hoped the exclusive would get him promoted."

Paige stared at Daniel, but clamped her lips together. Briony could tell she wanted to shout *I told you so* to her brother-in-law.

"Maybe the sisters discovered he'd lied about his true intentions and they don't like being lied to," Montague said dryly. "If he wrote, or threatened to expose secrets about Dark Hall and the psychic—"

"Medium," Daniel interrupted. "Sharlyn's a medium, not a psychic. There's a difference."

Montague appear unimpressed. "Uh-huh. As I was saying, if the *medium* feared negative attention or a police investigation into this so-called business of hers, she might have hired someone to shut Whealdon up for good. Or convinced her twin to plug him. I've heard twins have a bond that's unique to other sibling relationships. Even a special language, in some cases."

"Sharlyn wouldn't do such a thing," Daniel protested. "I've come to know her. She's as innocent as a lamb."

"Dressed in wolf's clothing," Paige mumbled.

Daniel's lips pursed. He looked like he wanted to tell Paige to shut up. He ground his fists into the chair cushion instead. Briony was on her friend's side. She didn't understand why Daniel was so strongly defending a woman he hardly knew, unless he was in love with her. Not only was Sharlyn blind, but so was love, as the saying went.

Mark finally chimed in. "I thoroughly read the newspaper every day, Sergeant. I haven't seen anything written about Dark Hall."

The policeman shrugged his broad shoulders. "It's just one theory. We have to start somewhere." He closed his notebook and stood up. His gaze met Daniel's. "If you learn anything new or learn the whereabouts of Shelby Dark, contact me immediately. I'll let you know when we get the fingerprint results back, or if we locate Shelby."

Daniel nodded and Mark showed the sergeant to the door. "Remember to stay low," he reminded Daniel before treading down the sidewalk.

When the door closed, the four of them stared at each other in silence. A few moments later, there was a knock. Sergeant Montague had returned. Mark welcomed him back inside.

"As soon as I got to my car, I received a call from headquarters on my radio. More interesting information has come to light with regard to Dark Hall. I'd recalled another case years ago that may have had some connection to Dark Hall, so I had my people go back and check our cold cases."

"Cold cases? What did your people find?" Briony asked.

"Five years ago, a man was discovered dead of a drug overdose in the red light district of town. Turns out he was a client of Sharlyn Dark's. According to the old files, those closest to him that were interviewed at the time mentioned that he'd gone to the mansion on numerous occasions. After a couple of months, he'd fancied himself personally involved with Miss Dark. In love, they said."

Briony glanced at Daniel. A strange intensity streamed from his eyes.

"Do you think that man was murdered?" Mark asked. "And his death might be connected with this one?"

"It's something we're going to dig into further." Montague snorted out short breaths, reminding Briony of a bull ready to charge. He glanced around Mark's shoulder and met Daniel's gaze. "Mr. Collier, take heed of my earlier warning. Steer clear of the Dark women until we know more about these two men and whether their connection is coincidence or concrete. If the twins are murderers, you have no idea what you're up against. You're already someone's target. Could be Shelby. Could be Sharlyn."

A vague nod tilted Daniel's head, and he sunk into a chair looking as if life had been drained out of him.

Once again, the sergeant bid them goodbye.

"This is too much," Paige cried, throwing herself into Mark's arms.

After a long awkward silence, Daniel stood up and walked toward the kitchen like he was in a trance.

"Where do you think you're going?" Mark shouted to his back and threw his hands into the air.

Briony followed Daniel into the kitchen. He ripped his fedora from the peg on the wall and jammed his arms into the sleeves of his winter coat. "You can't go back to Dark Hall," she said.

He fixed her with a stare so palpable it froze the muscles around her mouth.

"Try and stop me."

CHAPTER SEVEN

Briony was determined to do her best. She grabbed his arm. "You heard what the sergeant said. One or both of the twins could be murderers. You can't risk going to Dark Hall again."

Daniel stared at the hat in his hand and sighed. His mouth relaxed. "Why didn't Sharlyn tell us this morning that the police had questioned her last night?"

She shook her head. "I know you feel something for her, but I believe she's playing games. She could be hiding Shelby. In fact, I'd bet my life on it. I hope Sergeant Montague will be able to get a warrant to search Dark Hall."

He tossed the fedora onto the kitchen table, and his lips pulled back. "I shouldn't have gone to meet Shelby for drinks."

"Why did you?"

A bitter laugh escaped his throat. "I'm a fool. Aren't all men? I was immediately and profoundly attracted to her. She's unlike any other woman. And I've been lonely. I thought..." The obvious dangled on his lips.

Her disappointed gaze clamped onto him. "Shelby and Sharlyn are identical twins. How could you be attracted to one and not the other? Besides, I was under the impression you were in love with Sharlyn. Why would you take a chance at ruining something with her for one night with her sister?"

"You wouldn't understand. You're not a man. You don't have the urges and desires of a man. Shelby came across as a woman who wasn't afraid of those desires. Sharlyn, on the other hand, is an innocent. She's pure. Do you get my gist?"

Briony felt a blush creep back into her neck. "I think I do. However, I also think you're wrong about Shelby."

"What are you talking about?"

She didn't want to spell it out, but apparently, she'd have to. "In my opinion, Shelby only invited you to her place for drinks because I was with you and she hoped I'd come along."

His head angled, uncomprehending.

The blush warming her neck moved into her cheeks and flamed. "I don't think Shelby is interested in men, Daniel. You're an educated person. Surely you've read about homosexual relationships in literature."

When understanding lit his eyes, he threw his head back and laughed. "You thought Shelby was interested in *you*?"

"Is it so unbelievable?" Although unintentional, her voice cracked like a whip. "I'm not a slimy lagoon creature with scales and one big eye in the middle of my head, you know."

His laughter halted. "Of course you're not, Briony. You're quite a pretty girl, actually. But what makes you think Shelby was attracted to you and not me?"

"She flirted with me, Daniel. Blatantly. You were too mesmerized by her charming figure and sultry looks to notice, but it was obvious to me."

A muscle in his jaw ticked. "I thought those kind of women were masculine looking. I never would have guessed..."

"Don't be silly, Daniel. From what I understand, masculinity has nothing to do with it." An idea suddenly occurred to her. She snapped her fingers. "I just thought of something. What if Andrew Whealdon didn't show up on Shelby's steps by coincidence last evening? If Shelby and Sharlyn had figured out he was a reporter and was about to expose Sharlyn of fraud or pushing drugs, or whatever she's into—"

Daniel interceded. "Drugs? You now think Sharlyn is a drug dealer?"

"I'm only talking aloud as to the kinds of criminal activities a news reporter would want to uncover. Stop taking offense at everything I say about Sharlyn. I'm trying to figure out what's going on at Dark Hall and keep you from becoming its next victim."

Daniel snapped his mouth shut.

"Now, as I was saying... I wonder if Shelby contacted Andrew Whealdon yesterday after meeting us and asked him to meet her at the brownstone shortly before you were to show up at seven. She might have enticed him by suggesting she wanted to get back together. The perfect plan would be for her to kill him and then leave you unconscious next to his dead body. You'd be the perfect scapegoat."

Daniel shrugged. "Don't get offended, but your idea sounds a bit naïve. If that were her strategy, she would have placed the gun in my hand after knocking me unconscious. My fingerprints would have been all over the weapon, and I'd probably be in a holding cell right now charged with murder."

"Mmmm. That's true. There's definitely a learning curve that goes with detecting." Solving puzzles was difficult. She rubbed her temples. "I'm getting a headache."

He opened a cabinet door and handed her a bottle of aspirin. "I'm sorry to have gotten you involved in all of this. Thanks for trying to help. You're a good detective."

She popped two pills into her mouth and washed them down with tap water. "I appreciate the compliment." Her thoughts flashed to John. Even if she weren't quite Nancy Drew, wouldn't he be proud when she told him how her investigatory skills had improved?

From upstairs, they heard Amanda cry. "Excuse me, Daniel. What I need right now is to forget about murder and go cuddle that baby. But promise me something, will you?"

"What's that?"

"Stay home. Don't slip out when you think no one's looking. You might get yourself killed, and that would put a damper on Amanda's christening on Sunday."

He smiled his promise, and she went in search of Paige.

~ * ~

After feeding and playing with the baby, she helped Paige bake cookies for the christening brunch. Then she tried to rest. However, nightmares involving ghosts, blood, horned rams, and witches made for a disturbing nap.

When she woke, she slipped on a sweater and went downstairs. The house was quiet. Perhaps everyone else had nodded off, too. She stepped outside hoping the fresh air would chase the bad dreams from her mind. Colder than she expected, a stiff breeze sliced through her clothes. The sunless afternoon felt as cold as a witch's breath.

Although she'd come to Chicago to relax and spend time with Paige and her family, Briony had gotten involved in a mystery involving murder and some strange people living in a mansion. Now it was all she could think about. She'd awakened from the nap wondering how long it would take the police to get the fingerprint results back from the door and mail slot. She searched the dry ground around the front door for footprints, but of course, there were none.

A flock of birds scattered across the dull sky, reminding her of Maine and the seagulls that swooped and glided over the sea. A smile played on her lips as memories of John stirred within her. It had been a chilly autumn day when they'd first met on the ferry. It would be a wintry Valentine's weekend when they saw each other next. She'd always hated the cold. But if all went well with John next weekend, perhaps from now on she'd associate the coldest months of the year with him, making fall and winter her new favorite seasons. A heartstring vibrated in her chest, momentarily taking her mind off of Dark Hall and the trouble Daniel had found himself in.

From inside the house, she heard the telephone ring. Perhaps she should answer it, if everyone else was sleeping. She hurried through the door blowing on her hands to warm them and saw Daniel reach for the jingling phone. He smiled and nodded hello when he caught her eye.

"Hello, Collier residence. Yes, this is Daniel. Sharlyn! What a surprise." After a pause, his smile faded. "What's happened?"

Briony stepped closer to listen to the one-sided conversation.

"Shelby's at Dark Hall? What's going on? Who's screaming in the background?" Daniel listened for a moment, and his brows furrowed in confusion. "Griggs? Who the devil is Griggs?" As he waited for the answer, Briony could hear sobbing through the phone. "Griggs is the butler? What? Did you say he's taken poison?" Daniel's eyes enlarged.

Terror strummed Briony's nerves like a madman playing violin.

"Have you called an ambulance?" he asked. "Yes, yes. Stay calm. I'll be right over." He slammed down the receiver.

"That was Sharlyn? How was she able to dial the phone to call you?" Briony asked.

"I don't know. I suppose Shelby dialed for her. She's there."

I *knew* she'd try to hide at Dark Hall," Briony said, feeling her chest expand with satisfaction. "What on earth is going on?"

He plowed a hand through his hair. "The butler at Dark Hall has swallowed poison and left a suicide note, confessing to have murdered Andrew Whealdon, Todd Brandt, and Oliver Dark."

She gasped. "Who's Todd Brandt?"

"I have no idea, but Sharlyn is beside herself. She

was very close to the butler, apparently. I have to go. She needs my help."

"Wait." Briony gripped his arm. "Did they call the police and an ambulance?"

"I'm not sure. I could also hear a woman crying hysterically in the background. It must have been Shelby. They probably aren't thinking straight."

Conflicting emotions clawed at Broiny's stomach. Foreboding rose like a full moon. "I think we should call Sergeant Montague before we go. He can meet us at Dark Hall."

"We?"

"I can't let you go by yourself. But I'm scared. This could be a ploy. Remember, someone has threatened you. Most likely it was someone at Dark Hall. We need to contact the sergeant. The butler may not have committed suicide. It could be another murder. Or maybe he's not dead at all. Everyone in Dark Hall might be in a conspiracy together, or the girls might be faking their distress."

Daniel rolled his eyes. "If you'd heard the crying, you wouldn't think they were faking anything."

"Please," Briony said. "Listen to me. You're emotionally involved. I'm the voice of reason. Call Sergeant Montague."

He finally acquiesced and phoned police headquarters, but he left a message when told Montague was on another line.

"Let's wait until he returns your call," Briony begged.

"I can't wait. I'm leaving now. Montague will get my message and meet me there."

"If you insist. Wait for me to grab my coat."

He grabbed her arm. "No. You're staying here. Tell Mark and Paige what's going on. I can't involve you more than I already have. You're right about my feelings for Sharlyn. I love her, and I want to be there for her. She won't hurt me."

"But Shelby might!"

Ignoring her, he strode to the kitchen where his coat and hat were and flung the coat over his shoulders like Superman's cape.

Briony's heart thundered. Old fears stirred like a bear arousing from hibernation. It would be safer to stay here. But no detective worth her salt would let fear hold her back. Crimes weren't solved from the recliner. She'd grown so much in the past few months. Anxiety wouldn't defeat her now. Detecting seemed to have gotten into her blood. More importantly, she needed to keep Daniel from running off half-cocked to Dark Hall. He'd finally admitted he loved Sharlyn. But that didn't mean he'd be safe with her.

"I'm going. Wait for me!" she called, dashing out of the kitchen and up the stairs to her room. She pulled on her jacket and stuffed her feet into fur-lined boots. When she returned to the living room, Daniel had finished scribbling a note to Mark and Paige, which he left next to the telephone.

"Let's go," he said, casting open the front door.

It was a good thing she'd dressed warmly and put on boots. Fat flakes of snow were falling from the sky.

~ * ~

A thin layer of powdery snow covered the ground by the time they arrived at Dark Hall. An ambulance was parked in front, but no police vehicles. Daniel urgently pressed the buzzer next to the front door. After the third time, an unfamiliar masculine voice crackled through the intercom.

"Who's there?"

"Daniel Collier. Let me in."

"I don't know anyone by that name. Why are you here? Who called you?" The voice was tart and laced with suspicion.

"Sharlyn called me. Please let me in."

Silence met his plea. Exasperated, Daniel shouted into the intercom box. "Look. I know what happened to the butler. Sharlyn called and asked me to come. Now open up!"

The door finally creaked open. A handsome man looking to be in his late thirties or early forties stood erect on the other side. Strongly built with a flat nose and a full beard, he looked dapper in dress pants, a sports jacket, and a tie. His hair was curly and jet-black. Briony found herself staring at his large pointed ears. Memories of her studies in mythology flooded back.

This man resembled a Satyr! From what she remembered of Greek mythology from school, a Satyr had goat-like features and was a lover of wine and women. Satyrs were ready for every physical pleasure and were obsessed with nymphs, whom they often pursued through a ritualistic dance.

The weird tapestry she'd seen in the séance room of this mansion also flashed through her mind. A scream caught silently in her throat. This man didn't have horns like those rams gathered around the nude woman in the tapestry, but his dark eyes sparkled hypnotically like black diamonds. A shiver ran the length of her when he smiled and bared razor-sharp teeth. She entered the foyer squeezing close to Daniel.

"Who did you say you were?" The man's gaze raked them up and down.

"I'm Daniel Collier and this is Briony Martin. I told you over the intercom that I'm a friend of Sharlyn's. She phoned and told me what happened to the butler, Griggs. Is he going to survive?"

The man shook his head. "Sadly, he passed away ten minutes ago. The coroner has been contacted."

"The police are on their way, as well," Daniel said. "They should be here any minute."

The man's head snapped toward him with eyes flashing. His mouth opened and closed, as if he were about to comment and then changed his mind. Was there a reason he hadn't wanted the police called? Briony felt an emotional charge surge from her neck to her knees when his spellbinding gaze met hers.

"I didn't catch *your* name," Daniel said.

The man stuck out his hand to shake. "Nikolaos Yannatos."

"Isn't that Greek?" Briony asked, feeling her heart pound against her rib.

He stared. "Yes, it is. My ancestors came to this country many years ago."

"And how are you associated with Sharlyn and Shelby?" Daniel asked.

Yannatos's gaze narrowed. "I'm the Dark family's lawyer. I was the first person they called when Griggs was discovered in his quarters. I've known the girls all their lives. Oliver Dark's ancestors are also from the Old Country. He and I grew up together."

Briony bit her lip. She didn't believe it. If Oliver were still alive, he would probably be in his sixties. That would make Yannatos the same age and at least twenty years older than he looked. How could that be, unless he drank a magic potion that kept him immortal? Paige's talk about witchcraft and sorcery had gotten into her head. She shook it hard to rid herself of the ridiculous thought.

Daniel's chest swelled, and his chin lifted. "I want to see Sharlyn and Shelby. Will you please take us to them?"

Before Yannatos could answer, a whirring sound caught their attention. Briony recognized it as the elevator they'd taken to the second floor on the night of the séance. Two paramedics appeared from the dim hallway wheeling a gurney. The body stretched upon the gurney was covered with a white blanket. The paramedics halted in front of them.

"Mr. Yannatos, we'll be taking Mr. Griggs to the city morgue now," one of them said.

"Fine, thank you."

Daniel placed his hand on the cart to stop it from rolling. "No, it isn't fine. The Chicago police department is on their way. This man isn't going anywhere until they get here. They need to conduct an investigation, even if it's a suicide."

"I'm sure you know that's proper procedure," Briony added, glancing between the two paramedics. Sheepishly, they both looked at Yannatos for direction.

His lips were taut. "Of course." His head snapped toward the library. "You men can move the body into that room."

"Yes, sir," the medics said in unison.

Once they'd disappeared into the library, Daniel repeated, "Please take us to Sharlyn and Shelby."

Yannatos hesitated.

"What are you waiting for?"

"I think it would be better if you come back later when there's less chaos."

Daniel gritted his teeth in frustration. "We're not coming back later. I insist you take us to Sharlyn now! I love her. She needs me. I'm here to help her through this crisis."

"You love her?" Yannatos said, clearly surprised.

"Yes." Daniel's patience had run out. "If you won't show me to her, I'll find her myself." He began walking in circles around the foyer loudly shouting out her name. "Sharlyn! Sharlyn!"

"Stop," Yannatos said, clutching at his arm. "It's obvious you care for her."

"Damn right I do."

A long moment passed before the man spoke again. "I can also see you don't understand the situation."

Briony spoke up. "I think we do understand, Mr. Yannatos. Sharlyn's been hiding Shelby here since Andrew Whealdon was killed in her apartment. The police will want to question her when they arrive. Is that why you didn't call them about the butler's death? You don't want them to know it was Shelby and not Griggs who committed the crime. Am I correct?"

He said nothing, but she shuddered under his blue chill.

"As her lawyer, you must convince her to speak to them," she continued, willing her voice not to shake.

"Shelby won't be in trouble if she had nothing to do with the murder. But if she, or the twins together planned the crime, they must be held accountable."

Daniel moaned, "Briony, I told you Sharlyn isn't capable of killing anyone. She helps people, she doesn't hurt them."

"I'm sorry, Daniel, but a man was murdered in cold blood. Maybe even two men. And you were attacked. Whomever is responsible must face charges."

"You've got it all wrong," Yannatos said darkly. "Griggs left a note. He confessed to killing this Whealdon fellow, as well as a man named Todd Brandt five years ago, and my old friend, Oliver, ten years prior. Griggs wrote that Oliver didn't fall down the stairs. He pushed him. Griggs committed all the crimes."

"Why?" Briony asked. "What was his motive?"

"The note explained that he felt possessed by a demonic spirit. Many years ago, he'd spurned a woman. She was a witch and put a curse on him. From that moment on, he was consumed by satanic desires. Like a starving man craving a meal, his only gratification came when he killed. He fought hard to control his urges, but with this last kill, the guilt apparently became too much to live with any longer. He wanted to go to the police and confess what he'd done, but he was old and knew he wouldn't survive prison. His note said he decided suicide was his best option."

"A witch!" Daniel exclaimed. "Of all the ridiculous things…" He shook his head, unbelieving. "The police will want to see that suicide note."

"What a tall tale," Briony muttered, "even for a bizarre place like Dark Hall. It's my opinion something less theatrical, but far more sinister is at play here. Would you like to hear my theory, Mr. Yannatos?"

He clasped his hands behind his back. "I suppose I have no choice." His cold stare turned her body to ice.

She inhaled deeply. "I do think someone in this house killed Andrew Whealdon, Todd Brandt, and maybe even Oliver Dark. But it wasn't Griggs. However, Griggs knew who that person was. Perhaps he's been covering for her all these years. After Whealdon was found dead in Shelby's brownstone, he knew the police were closing in on the real murderer, so he asked her to turn herself in. She refused and murdered him to keep him from spilling the truth."

"Preposterous. Who *are* you, anyway?" Yannatos tossed his hand into the air. "Tell me why I shouldn't throw the two of you out on the step right now?"

"Because you know I'm right, Mr. Yannatos. Griggs did not commit suicide. You're a lawyer who has sworn to uphold justice. You can't do that and keep protecting the twins. It's time for the truth to come out."

His mouth twisted. "You have no idea what you're talking about."

"Then tell us what's really going on. Take us to the girls," Daniel demanded.

Yannatos spun on his heel. "Very well. Follow me. If you want the truth, you'll get it."

CHAPTER EIGHT

His shiny patent leather shoes clicked along the floor as Briony and Daniel trailed him past the spiral staircase to the hallway where the elevator was located. Head craned over her shoulder, her gaze moved to the top of the glass dome above the winding stairs. She doubted anyone could have survived a fall, or push, down those stairs. Least of all, an older man Oliver Dark's age. Why had he been on the stairs at all, when there was an elevator in the mansion? She wondered if he'd been lured there.

Without speaking, the three of them rode the elevator up to the third floor. The door slid open. As they padded down a hallway of thick carpet, Briony found the stillness odd. She'd heard sobbing on the phone when Daniel was speaking to Sharlyn. And he'd said a woman was crying hysterically in the background. Had the mourning stopped so suddenly? Or was this a ruse as she'd first suspected?

Myriad thoughts flashed through her mind. Was Yannatos in cahoots with the twins? Knowing Daniel had been speaking to the police, had they lured him here to silence him for good this time? If so, they'd have to get rid of her, too. At least Daniel had left Mark and Paige a note. It was some consolation the couple would have proof of Briony and Daniel's destination to show police if they turned up missing, or worse.

The lawyer stopped in front of a walnut paneled door. Without knocking, he opened it. "This is Sharlyn's room," he said, stepping back to allow Daniel and Briony to look inside. As she expected, it was eclectically decorated in feminine colors and fabrics mixed with an assortment of objects related to the supernatural. Some of the things she noted as her gaze perused the room were a large crystal ball, Tarot cards, bottles of oils, incense sticks, candles, and a Ouija board.

"Sharlyn isn't here," Yannatos said.

"That's obvious," Daniel stated dryly.

Yannatos closed the door and moved further down the hall. After stopping at another door, he opened it, also without bothering to knock. "This is Shelby's room, when she's around."

They peeked inside. It reeked of strong perfume and resembled a bordello, or at least what Briony imagined a bordello to look like.

"Shelby's not here, either," the lawyer said.

"We can see that," Daniel thundered. "What game are you playing?"

Yannatos shut the door. His burning hot gaze seared two holes through Daniel. "This is no game, Mr. Collier." He set his shoulders and clenched his teeth. "If only it were. You did say you're in love with Sharlyn, didn't you?"

"Yes, I am."

"But you were also captivated by and physically attracted to Shelby when you met her? Am I correct?"

Briony saw Daniel's Adam's apple slide up and down his throat. "That's none of your business. What are you driving at?" he said, angrily.

The corner of Yannatos's mouth turned up, and his fang-like tooth glistened. "They're as different as fire and ice, but men are always falling in love with both of them. There's something oddly provocative about twins, don't you agree?" His eyebrow cocked.

"What in the hell are you prattling on about?" Daniel said. "You're very close to sounding perverted. If you don't watch your mouth, I may have to punch it."

"You, Mr. Collier, are no different from all the others. You were a fool to get mixed up with any of them."

Any of them? The air in the hall suddenly grew thick. It was hard for Briony to breathe. Her mind clouded over. She tried desperately to grasp the man's meaning, but her logical brain refused to accept his implication.

Yannatos ignored Daniel's threat and strode to the end of the hall and stopped. "This is Shawna's room. When I introduce you, try to hide your shock. It could be devastating for her if you don't." He knocked on the door and then turned his watchful eyes on them as if expecting them to make a run for it.

"Who the hell is Shawna?" Daniel croaked.

Standing beside her, Briony could sense his tense muscles practically bursting through his clothes. Her heart pounded with an insane rhythm. She stared at Yannatos. His mesmerizing eyes sparkled wickedly, and the blinders fell from her eyes. Her body went numb. If only she'd been more perceptive all along! But she'd been as sightless as Sharlyn.

"Come in," a voice called.

Yannatos pushed open the door and the three of them stepped inside. There she was standing in the middle of the room. Briony gazed around quickly. It was the room of a teenage girl, with clothes scattered on the floor, the bed unmade, and rock and roll music playing from a transistor radio.

"Shawna, please turn the music off," Yannatos requested.

She did so and stepped forward and sighed. "Hello, Nickolaos." The words were not spoken in Sharlyn's sweet, bewitching tone nor in Shelby's seductive voice, but with the intonation of a bored teenager who didn't want to be bothered. Her long hair was pulled into two braids, and despite the cold weather, she wore Capri pants and a short-sleeved top that accentuated her soft curves. Her head angled.

"We have guests," Yannatos told her. "Do you recognize these people, my dear?"

The woman with both Sharlyn and Shelby's face rudely chomped on the gum inside her mouth and shook her head. "Nope. Should I?"

This was neither Sharlyn nor Shelby, but someone else altogether. Shawna, the lawyer had said. Briony flicked a glance at Daniel. From the petrified expression on his face, she thought he understood. Or maybe he didn't understand at all.

"Are these people doctors?" Shawna asked. "Are they here about Griggs?"

"No, my dear," Yannatos replied. "They're not doctors. They're friends of Sharlyn and Shelby."

"Oh." Her face went blank. "I heard them crying a while ago. Has something dreadful happened to Griggs?"

He reached out to pat her arm. "We'll talk about all that later, Shawna. Say goodbye to these nice people."

"Goodbye," she said, turning her back on them. Daniel exited the room behind Yannatos trudging out like a war-wounded soldier. Before Briony followed, she watched Shawna flick the transistor back on and start dancing. When she twirled and caught Briony watching, she stuck her tongue out and marched forward and slammed the door in her face.

The three of them stepped into the elevator. They rode it in silence to the ground floor. Briony ached for the depth of pain that filled Daniel's face.

Once they'd reached the foyer, he asked, "Are they triplets? Or..."

She remembered the advertisement about a movie that had been released at the end of last year starring Joanne Woodward, but she hadn't seen it. The film was called *The Three Faces of Eve*. With her heart hammering, she searched Yannatos's face. He nodded at her. "You understand, don't you?"

She returned a curt nod. "Sharlyn, Shelby, and Shawna. They're all one person."

"It's called Multiple Personality Disorder."

But which was her true identity? Briony wondered.

Daniel's forehead crinkled in confusion. "But how is such a thing possible? Has she been possessed by a demon? It must have something to do with her communicating with spirits."

"Don't be ridiculous," Yannatos gritted. "You've seen with your own eyes, but you refuse to believe. There are no satanic forces at work. The child is mentally ill."

"Has she seen a doctor?" Briony asked.

"Yes, there have been many medical doctors and psychiatrists who have tested her through the years. They've all said the same thing. She inherited her poor mother's disease of the mind. Oliver's daughter, Bella, has been committed to an insane asylum since Sharlyn was a toddler."

"How awful. Is Sharlyn her true identity?" Briony asked.

"That's the name she was given at birth, yes. And her sweet personality is authentic. But as the other two personas began to emerge and develop their own characteristics when she was younger, Sharlyn took on one unique trait."

"She's not blind, you mean," Daniel said, stone-faced.

"That's correct."

"Is she a medium? Or is that all a hoax, too?"

"The ability to connect with the dead seemed to correlate with when she claimed to first lose her sight. That was about five years ago."

"Around the same time Todd Brandt was discovered to have overdosed after becoming involved with Sharlyn," Briony noted.

Yannatos's lips thinned. He was a lawyer and knew his rights. He wasn't going to say anything more that would possibly incriminate his client, and probably knew he'd said too much already.

A fist pounded on the front door at the same time the buzzer sounded. Briony recognized the voice that came through the intercom speaker.

"That's Sergeant Montague," Daniel said. When

Yannatos hesitated, he said, "If you don't open the door, I will. The police are coming in one way or the other."

The lawyer unlocked the door. In stepped Montague, one uniformed policeman, a man carrying a black medical bag, and another man in a rumpled trench coat and fedora. "I got your message," the sergeant said to Daniel. He introduced the man in the trench coat and then the man carrying the bag. "This is Detective Bailey of the homicide division, and this is Dr. Hamel. Where's the suicide victim?"

With his pupils squinted into pinpoints, Yannatos introduced himself and motioned in the direction of the library. "Two paramedics are waiting for permission to take the body to the coroner's office."

"The body shouldn't have been moved," Montague said gruffly.

"Where was he found?" Bailey inquired.

"Lying on his bed in his room at the back of the house."

"Was there a suicide note?"

"Yes. It's still sitting on the bedside table, along with the half-empty glass of milk he apparently mixed the poison in. Nothing's been touched."

The cords on the sergeant's neck flexed and quivered. "Except the body itself."

"I phoned Dr. Crisman," Yannatos defended. "He wasn't able to leave his office and said he'd send an ambulance."

"That's not protocol and the coroner knows it," Montague thundered.

Yannatos's voice was measured. "I apologize, Sergeant. The man has been the butler of Dark Hall for over forty years. I was trying to save additional distress to those in the household. It was quite a shock to all of us. His name is George Griggs."

"We know his name," Montague said. "I've spoken to Dr. Crisman myself. That's why Dr. Hamel is here." His head jerked toward one of the policemen. "Officer Drake, go to the library and instruct the medics to move the gurney to another part of the house where Dr. Hamel can conduct an examination."

"Yes sir."

"Where's the best place for them to go?" the sergeant asked Yannatos.

"I suppose the salon would work." When Drake exited the library moments later with the paramedics pushing the gurney, he directed them to the salon.

"We'll be waiting in the library," Montague told the detective and the doctor.

When they'd gone, he turned his attention back to Briony, Daniel, and Yannatos. "We've just finished interviewing the coroner, and he was very helpful in clearing up a few things. Turns out, he keeps piss-poor records in that office of his, but when strongly encouraged, the man has a memory like an elephant. With a little prodding, he was able to recall details of cases dating back five, ten years even." The corner of his lip lifted in a sly smile.

"What sort of things?" Yannatos asked, wringing his hands.

"Things involving the people of Dark Hall. But we'll get to all that soon enough. Right now, I want you to bring everyone in this house downstairs. I need to interview them."

Exhilaration coursed through Briony's veins. The

air buzzed with nervous energy. Finally, there were going to be answers to all her questions.

Yannatos's eyes widened. "There's no one else in the mansion except Miss Dark and her assistant. It's the housekeeper's day off. The valets are only here on nights when séances are held. There hasn't been a large staff serving Dark Hall in years."

"Which Miss Dark are you referring to?" the sergeant asked.

Sweat glowed across Yannatos's upper lip. "Miss Sharlyn Dark."

"Shelby is not currently here at Dark Hall?"

"Not to my knowledge," he answered.

Biony and Daniel exchanged a glance. Montague shrugged, off-handedly. "Then bring Miss Dark and her assistant to the library."

The visibly anxious Greek lawyer disappeared into the hallway, and they heard the whir of the elevator as it ascended.

Briony wondered which Miss Dark would actually appear before the sergeant. Yannatos had said it would be Sharlyn. Could she alter her persona on a whim? Or did some outside influence or emotional disturbance trigger the change? She could tell by the soft groan that tore from Daniel's chest that the same question haunted him. She speculated on whether it would be best to warn the sergeant about Sharlyn's different personalities or let him find out for himself. Daniel's lip stayed buttoned. If he wasn't going to say anything, neither would she.

"Did the coroner shed any light on the death of Oliver Dark?" she asked instead.

"Still playing private eye, I see, Miss Martin." A

deep chuckled rumbled from Montague's belly. "All in good time. Let's go into the library, shall we?"

Obviously, he wasn't prepared to discuss with her and Daniel what he knew or didn't know. She followed the two men into the library and sat on the far side of the room where she fixed her gaze upon the blazing fire someone had made in the hearth.

Montague lowered his weight into a Victorian parlor chair.

It was fifteen minutes before Yannatos entered the library. Briony's gaze lifted. On the lawyer's arm was Sharlyn, looking as beautiful as ever dressed in a flowing white dress and staring straight ahead with her blue eyes wide open. Behind them shadowed her assistant, dressed casually in trousers and a pullover shirt. Lee's eyes were swollen and rimmed in red.

"Have a seat," Sergeant Montague said. Sharlyn and Lee sat side-by-side on the settee with Yannatos in a chair next to them. Having met before, Montague abandoned the formality of a re-introduction. "I'm sorry for your loss. I understand the butler had been with the family for forty years."

"That's correct," Sharlyn replied, softly. She dabbed her nose with a tissue.

Briony stood up and quietly took a seat next to Daniel. His steady gaze never left Sharlyn's face. Once, she turned her head and looked at him. "Daniel, are you here?"

"Yes, but how did you know?"

"I smell your cologne." Her angelic smile could have melted ice.

Montague got straight to the point. "Miss Dark, are you hiding your sister, Shelby, here at Dark Hall?"

"No, Sergeant. I haven't seen my sister in over six months. She has a brownstone downtown and lives a fast life."

"That's a lie, and I know it." His mouth pressed into a straight line.

"Say now," Yannatos cut in, frowning.

"Shut up," Montague barked, causing Briony to jump. "I'm interviewing Miss Dark. Not you. Now, Miss Dark, are you aware that a man by the name of Andrew Whealdon was found murdered in Shelby's brownstone?"

"Yes...yes, I am," she stammered. "I knew Andrew. He was a client of mine. Nice fellow."

"Yes, he was a client of yours, and you introduced him to your sister three months ago, yet you claim not to have seen Shelby in six months. How does that add up?"

She folded her hands into her lap. "I must be mistaken about the time period. I apologize."

Lee stared at her own hands in her lap. Her lips visibly trembled.

"Does your sister own a gun?" the sergeant asked.

"I have no idea."

"What about you? Are you the registered owner of a firearm?"

A smug smile played across her lips. "That might lead to a dangerous situation, Sergeant. In case you hadn't noticed, I'm blind."

He retrieved a piece of paper from his pocket. "Then how is it I have a copy of a permit with your name on it originally dated May 1952 and renewed in 1955?"

She didn't skip a beat. "I don't know, Sergeant.

Doesn't a person have to complete a firearm safety course before being allowed to purchase a gun?"

"Yes."

She chuckled. "I couldn't possibly pass a safety course in my condition. More than likely, my sister pretended to be me. Don't ask me why. She's always had a macabre sense of humor. Or perhaps her unsavory dealings in the past didn't allow her to pass a background check. We're identical twins. It would be easy for her to forge my signature and buy a gun."

"But not as easy for her to forge your fingerprints. Every person who registers for a firearm has his or her fingerprints placed on file. Twins don't have the same fingerprints, even identical twins." When a gasp caught in her throat, he added, "I'm not as dumb as I look."

"I can't see how you look," Sharlyn said, quietly.

"Oh, I think you can," Montague replied.

Not a muscle moved in Sharlyn's body. Lee squeezed her eyes shut. Briony noticed her hand shook when she grasped for Sharlyn's.

Even though the room was full of people, Montague leaned forward, assuming a confidential air. Then he dropped a bomb. "It's time to stop lying, Miss Dark. *Your* fingerprints are on file. Not Shelby's."

CHAPTER NINE

Deafening silence filled the room.

When the sergeant finally spoke again, his voice was low. "Sharlyn, we found the handgun that killed Andrew Whealdon. Your prints are all over it."

"No! They couldn't be."

Yannatos's hand snaked out to grab her wrist. "Don't say another word, Sharlyn. As your lawyer, I'm advising you to be quiet."

"But I didn't kill that man," she said, ignoring his counsel.

"You killed him *and* Todd Brandt," Montague argued. "We have evidence and a confession that proves you administered Brandt a lethal dose of cocaine. And we also know you murdered your own grandfather by pushing him down the stairs in this very mansion. Dr. Crisman has admitted to helping cover up both crimes. He's a greedy son-of-a-gun who has a hefty bank account and appears to have enjoyed a number of vacations in Europe, all bankrolled by your family. There's no use in denying any of it."

"But I—"

"Sharlyn, don't speak!" Yannatos exclaimed.

At that pivotal moment, Detective Bailey strode through the library door with Dr. Hamel on his heels. Montague's head jerked toward them. "What's the news, gentlemen?"

Dr. Hamel answered. "It wasn't suicide, Sergeant. George Griggs was murdered."

"Murdered! It's not possible." Yannatos hung his head in his hands.

Briony saw Daniel stiffen. She, herself, struggled to find air.

Montague's nostrils flared. He stared into Sharlyn's eyes. "I have every reason to believe you killed the butler because he was about to implicate you. You committed three murders already and tried to put the blame on your twin, but Griggs knew the truth. Isn't that right? Why did you hate Shelby so much?"

Sharlyn shook her head, and tears sprang into her eyes.

"Interest in the debate about capital punishment has resurfaced," Montague threatened. "By the time your case goes to trial, the death sentence may be in place again. But if you confess and cooperate with us, I'll do what I can to recommend to the courts that you're granted a life sentence." His large hand covered her knee, a sympathetic gesture most likely used to play on her emotions.

Lee's eyes popped open. "Don't touch her!" she hissed, clawing at the sergeant's hand. He jerked his hand back. Detective Bailey lunged forward, but Montague waved him off. Frown lines appeared between his brows.

"Leave her alone!" Lee shouted. "She didn't kill any of them, but especially not Griggs. She'd never hurt him."

Briony's heart galloped inside at the turn of events. She looked at Daniel. His pallor was tinged with gray.

"But *you'd* hurt him if pushed into a corner, wouldn't you, Miss Leonti?" Montague baited.

The muscles around her mouth twitched. "Leonti? I'm not Miss Leonti. My name is Lee, and I wouldn't hurt Griggs either." She and Sharlyn clasped hands tightly.

"Stop playing games with me," Montague shouted. "You may pretend to be a man, but that doesn't make you one."

She flinched and then broke down. Her shoulders shook with sobs. It took several long moments before she could speak. "Please leave Sharlyn alone. I'm the one you want. She didn't kill anyone. She couldn't. She's too sweet and pure." Their gazes met, and it was obvious from the darting movement of her pupils that Sharlyn searched Lee's face and gazed lovingly into her eyes.

"Stop the B.S.," Montague bellowed. "I don't know why you're playing this sick game, but your name is Cathy Leonti and your mother was the former housekeeper of Dark Hall, before she passed away of cancer eleven years ago. Did you think we wouldn't find out?"

Lee's muted sobs tapered off and finally stopped, replaced by bodily fatigue that seemed to have zapped her of all energy. She leaned into Sharlyn's ear and whispered something into it.

"No, Lee." Sharlyn's voice was soft. Her lips trembled.

"Yes. I can't let you go to prison for what I did. It'll be okay. Trust me, as you always have." She released Sharlyn's hand and stared at Montague. The room was as hushed as fallen snow. She licked her lips, gulped, and began her confession.

"I murdered Oliver Dark ten years ago by shoving him down the spiral staircase. I did it because he abused me when I was a girl, and I found out he'd started up with Sharlyn. By the time she confided in me, I was already dressing like a male. I thought my becoming a boy would keep that dirty old man away from me. And it worked. But I had no idea he'd go after his own granddaughter." Her eyes narrowed with fury at the memory. "I was determined not to let him hurt her the way he hurt me. Sharlyn and I grew up in this house together. I love her. I've always protected her, and I always will."

Montague cast a quick glance at Detective Bailey, who was taking notes. "And Todd Brandt? Why did you kill him?"

"He used Sharlyn, just like all men use women. The man was a drug addict. I didn't think anyone would miss him."

"Andrew Whealdon? What did he do to deserve getting shot?"

Lee's shoulders hitched in a slight shrug. "He was going to tell terrible lies about Sharlyn."

"What about me?" Daniel asked. "You knocked me unconscious. But did you intend on killing me, too?"

An evil leer filled her face. "Yes. Guess I'm losing my touch."

Briony saw Daniel flinch with shock. "But why?" he wanted to know.

"You've grown too close to Sharlyn. I could see you wanted her for yourself. But she's mine, and the two of us don't need men. We don't want men and their dirty paws touching us. You're all a bunch of filthy animals."

An eerie stillness swallowed the room for what seemed an eternity. Montague finally broke the silence. "Where's Shelby, Cathy? Did you murder her, too?"

Briony glanced up from staring at her hands, startled. The sergeant apparently knew everything except Dark Hall's biggest secret.

Nickolaos Yannatos stood up wearily. "Shelby's safe, Sergeant. I'll explain it to you after you've read Cathy her rights."

Lee's confused gaze darted to the sergeant. "You said Sharlyn's fingerprints were found on the gun. But they couldn't be."

"They aren't." His eyebrow lifted slyly. "Stand up and place your hands behind your back." He snapped a pair of handcuffs on her. "Cathy Leonti, I'm arresting you for the murders of Oliver Dark, Todd Brandt, and Andrew Whealdon, as well as charging you with aggravated battery upon Daniel Collier."

After he read her the Miranda rights, Lee sniffled. "Who killed my grandfather? I didn't. I swear. I loved him. He was good to us, all of us."

Montague nodded. "I know. I suspect Mr. Griggs did commit suicide to protect you. Dr. Hamel will confirm the cause of death. Griggs probably thought his confession note would be the only thing the police would need to close the cases on those three murders."

"The butler was her grandfather?" Briony said.

"Yes, Miss Martin. The former housekeeper was Mary Leonti. She did die of cancer. Her maiden name was Griggs."

Lee's gaze narrowed into pinpricks and shifted from Montague to Detective Bailey and finally to Dr. Hamel. "You said my grandfather was murdered, but you all lied."

Montague offered no excuse. Briony knew deceit had been the only means with which to get at the truth. He directed the paramedics to take the butler's body to the city morgue and thanked Dr. Hamel for his time and assistance. "Detective Bailey, will you please escort Miss Leonti outside and into the squad car?"

Lee collapsed and had to be helped out of the room. She was so overwrought with emotion, she couldn't even utter a goodbye to Sharlyn. When they'd gone, Montague and Yannatos stepped to the far side of the room and spoke in quiet tones, where apparently, the lawyer explained Sharlyn's mental condition. Briony saw Montague plow a hand through his hair and shake his head in disbelief.

All this time, Sharlyn had sat quietly on the settee looking like a lost lamb. A tear slid down her cheek. Briony's heart swelled for her.

From across the room, the sergeant motioned to Daniel. He stepped toward him. Briony heard Montague say, "Mr. Collier, someone from my department will call you to let you know the status of Miss Leonti's case. You'll, of course, be testifying at the trial."

When the two men continued in hushed conversation, Briony sat next to Sharlyn and decided to bring up the subject that had been on her mind since the night of the séance.

"Sharlyn, it's Briony Martin here. I'm sorry about your friend, Lee, and Mr. Griggs."

"Thank you, Miss Martin. I'm not sure what I'm going to do without them. They've always been here for me. I'm going to feel so lost. I'll be alone."

Briony's heart squeezed. "You'll still have your work and your clients."

"I suppose so."

Briony understood how her interest for helping others might have diminished. "Miss Dark, may I ask you a direct question about your ability to communicate with the deceased?"

Sharlyn turned her body towards her. Their gazes connected, and the light in her eyes rekindled. "Certainly, Miss Martin."

A knot twisted Briony's stomach. "Please be honest with me. The night I attended your séance, how did you know I had a twin brother named Ben? Did Daniel call ahead of time and tell you?"

Her voice was soft. "No, Miss Martin. My gift is channeling loved ones that have passed over. I discovered I had the ability to do so when I was thirteen years old. That's also when I lost my sight."

It was also when your friend discovered your grandfather had been assaulting you, Briony thought with sadness.

"You miss him," Sharlyn stated. "Your brother, Ben. Although it was a tragedy, his death was an accident. I saw the drowning through his eyes. He didn't suffer. His lungs filled with water and he passed quickly."

The breath locked deep inside Briony's throat. How could Sharlyn have known Ben had drowned? Paige hadn't told Daniel those details.

"You left the circle before Ben could relate his

message," Sharlyn continued. "But I remember what he wanted you to know. Would you like me to tell you now?"

What could it hurt? "All right."

Sharlyn folded Briony's hand into hers. "He's proud of the way you've faced your fears. He sees that as a great accomplishment. And he's glad love has come into your life. He's happy because you're happy."

Tears threatened to burst from Briony's eyes. There's no way Sharlyn could have known those things about her. Even if she came by her ability through trauma and believed herself to be blind, she really could see into the world beyond. Briony was no longer a skeptic.

She composed herself and glanced over to see that Daniel was still speaking to the sergeant. "Thank you for sharing that with me, Miss Dark. There's one other thing I'd like to ask you about before I go. Nickolaos Yannatos."

Sharlyn's featherly light eyebrow lifted. "What about him?"

"He's alluded to his age as being in the sixties, but he appears much younger. And his looks are so unique. He reminds me of the powerful Greek mythological creatures I studied in school. I've been thinking he must have made a pact with the devil to stay so vigorous and young." She tried to chuckle away the nervous pitch of her voice.

Sharlyn's voice dropped conspiratorially low. "Nickolaos is a lawyer. All lawyers believe they're powerful, do they not? In fact, most of them have such a high opinion of themselves they practically think they're gods." She laughed, but there was a false note in her mirth.

She bent her head toward Briony. "In all seriousness, since you've asked, you might find it interesting to learn that Nickolaos is a member of a distinct Greek order that's been in existence since the sixteenth century. My grandfather also belonged. The details regarding the group's rituals and obligations are all very clandestine. But for centuries, there have been rumors of witchcraft being involved in their ceremonies. So I suspect your perception of our resident Greek isn't far off track."

Goosebumps peppered Briony's skin. She shook Sharlyn's hand and said goodbye. "Take care, and good luck." Realizing Sergeant Montague had left, she strolled over to Yannatos. Daniel excused himself and returned to Sharlyn's side.

"What will happen to her now?" Briony asked the lawyer.

"I'll see that she gets the psychiatric attention she needs. Cathy wouldn't allow me to before. She didn't trust any men and only tolerated my occasional presence because I still handle the taxes and other legal transactions with regard to Dark Hall."

"You won't put Sharlyn in an institution like her mother, will you?"

"I'll work closely with the doctors and avoid it, if at all possible."

"Please try your best." She felt on the verge of tears. "What happened to her wasn't her fault." After hearing what Sharlyn just said about his possible involvement in witchcraft, she allowed her suspicious gaze to roam over his features. "You told us you were

Oliver Dark's friend. You didn't know what he was doing to those girls when they were young?"

Yannatos heaved a deep sigh that seemed genuine. "If I had, I would have killed him myself."

She turned to see Daniel kiss Sharlyn on the cheek and walk away. Sharlyn smiled into the air and then closed her eyes and lowered her head. The whole scene had been one big melodrama, but now it was over. Briony was exhausted.

When she and Daniel stepped outside the front door, the snow had stopped falling, but the howling of the wind was frightful. She dove into the passenger side of the car and wrapped her arms around herself. It took several turns of the key before the cold vehicle roared to life. As the car sat shuddering, a feeling like someone was watching made Briony turn her head. The drapes in a downstairs window parted slightly. A figure in white stood at the pane, and a flash of blue eyes sparkled from behind the glass. Briony swallowed a sharp cry when a shadow from behind touched the woman's shoulder and wheeled her away from the window.

As Daniel slowly drove down the snow-packed driveway, Briony craned her head over the seat. It would be the last time she laid eyes on Dark Hall. A strange sense of paranoia rendered her transfixed. She kept her sight on the mansion until they passed through the gate. Then, with a knot in her stomach, she flipped around and huddled in the seat. Despite warm air blowing from the heater vents, the chill refused to leave her body.

~ * ~

Although the winter air was crisp on the day of the christening, the sun slanted brilliantly across the Chicago landscape, melting most of the snow. Amanda was baptized with Briony and Daniel promising to uphold their duties as godparents. Afterwards, friends and family gathered at the Collier home for refreshments.

When the busy day finally ended, Briony retreated to the spare room to pack. She was leaving early the next morning. A knock sounded on the door.

"Come in."

Paige stepped in, looking tired but happy. She sat on the edge of the bed. "It was a beautiful ceremony, wasn't it?"

"Yes." Briony smiled and halted her packing. "Thank you for making me Amanda's godmother. I love her to death, and I'm so glad I was able to share you and Mark's joy today."

"There wouldn't have been anyone else I'd choose. I trust you with my own life, Briony. I certainly trust you with my daughter's, should anything happen to Mark and I."

"Nothing's going to happen," she assured.

Paige's hand covered hers. "I want to apologize again for all you went through with Daniel and those people at Dark Hall. I never should have gotten you mixed up in it."

"It's over and done. There's no need to fret on my account. All of life is a learning experience."

"What do you think about Daniel? I'm still worried about him."

"Give him time. Naturally, he's a little sad because he did care for Sharlyn and thought their relationship might go somewhere. But I believe he'll be okay. When it's the right time, he'll meet someone wonderful and this experience will become one of many memories that will have helped him on his way to true happiness. You'll see."

"I hope you're right." Paige changed the subject abruptly. "Are you excited about John coming to visit next weekend?" She chortled. "What am I talking about? Of course, you must be dancing a jig inside."

"I am. I hope he still likes me after not seeing me for three months."

"What's not to like? You're the best person I know. Besides, if he didn't like you, he wouldn't be flying all the way from Maine to Kansas, and on Valentine's weekend, no less. I can't wait to hear what he gives you as a present."

Briony felt a blush creep into her cheeks. "I doubt he'll give me anything for Valentine's Day. We're not exactly sweethearts. He hasn't told me he loves me."

Paige winked. "He may be waiting for just the right occasion. It wouldn't be romantic to say *I love you* for the first time over the phone. The first time your soul mate tells you he loves you, you want those three little words to be accompanied by a passionate kiss."

"Soul mate. I like the sound of that." They giggled like the schoolgirls they used to be. Then Paige hugged her friend and said good night. Their time together had come to an end.

CHAPTER TEN

Briony had been home only one hour when the telephone rang. "I'll get it," she called to her mother. She nearly slipped on the floor rug as she ran to the den to grab the receiver. The beats of her heart picked up their pace when she heard John's deep voice on the other end.

"Welcome home, world traveler."

She chuckled. "Thank you, John. I'm not quite a world traveler yet, but maybe someday. At least my knuckles didn't turn white when I got on the plane this morning. That's progress."

He laughed, and she felt electrified while imagining his dark eyes and his crooked smile.

"Are you ready for me to invade your life next Friday?" he asked.

"I'm counting the days and minutes. Do you know your flight schedule yet?"

"Yep." As if he had it memorized, he told her the flight number and the time he'd be arriving at the airport.

"Perfect. I'm off work at four o'clock, so you won't have to take a taxi. I'll be there to meet you. Mom wants to make a special dinner that night. Do you mind? She's looking forward to getting to know you."

"I'm in your hands for the weekend, Briony. I'm

fine with whatever you want to do, except for Saturday night. I've got a special surprise planned for just the two of us."

Saturday was Valentine's Day. A pleasant sensation rolled through her torso and her heart beat faster. "I like surprises."

"Good. I hope you'll love this one."

"You're being so mysterious."

"Mysterious is my middle name."

Every nerve in her body tingled. If she didn't switch the subject, she just might swoon. "Do you know where you're staying in Wichita?"

"I've made a reservation at the Starlite Motor Lodge and Motel."

"That's great! It's not far from our house."

"I know. That's why I chose it. I want to be as close to you as possible." His voice was thick with emotion. It touched her. "I'll see you soon, Briony. And this time I mean it."

"Soon," she repeated. Although she wished he could stay longer than a weekend, she felt grateful for the little bit of time they'd have together. Anyway, she'd already used her vacation hours to go to Maine and now Chicago. No matter how badly she wanted to play hostess, she couldn't take more days off from work.

She returned the receiver to its cradle, and a shriek of pure joy gave wings to her feet. As she bounded up the stairs two steps at a time, she knew there was no need for a clairvoyant to tell her next weekend would be the best of her life.

~ * ~

The days couldn't pass fast enough. The moment Briony saw John saunter through the airport gate, her heart skittered to a stop. Seeing him before he saw her, she drew in a deep breath. He was dressed in denims and black boots and a heavy wool coat. A duffle bag was slung over his shoulder. His hair was still styled in the pompadour she loved.

Their gazes fused. His mouth broadened into a smile, and they waved at each other. His long-legged strides ate up the space between them. Standing in front of her, his dark eyes smoldered with an intense hunger. Without a thought to the people around them, he dropped the duffle bag on the ground and whisked her into his arms.

A thrill raced down her spine. "You're really here." He burrowed his face in her neck, and his warm breath tickled.

"Did you have doubts?" he asked, setting her back. She shook her head, and they stared into each other's eyes. Unexpectedly, he covered her lips with his. Although she'd been raised to believe a public display of affection was unbefitting, Briony ignored her mother's voice in her head. John was an unconventional man with a fierce passion for life. She met his passion, and a soft groan tore from his chest as he deepened the kiss. Despite the chill inside the airline terminal, she felt every inch of his warmth radiate through their clothes and into her body.

"I've missed you," he said, when their mouths parted.

"I've missed you, too."

He lifted the duffle bag from the ground and wrapped his arm around her waist. It was impossible to wipe the smile from her face as they made their way to the parking lot.

John climbed into the Buick and tossed his bag into the backseat. Dizzy with excitement, Briony jammed the key into the ignition. She couldn't believe he was sitting in the car next to her. Worry that their months apart might have stifled their new relationship melted like snow on a hot roof.

He grinned at her. "Can you talk and drive at the same time?"

"Of course," she chuckled. "I'm an excellent driver."

"Good, because I want you to tell me all about your experience in Chicago."

~ * ~

The next day, Briony drove John around town showing him the sights, such as the Orpheum Theatre, the historical museum, the zoo, and the courthouse where she worked. It gave them alone time away from the house. While she tooled them around the city, they talked about everything under the sun. Although they came from different worlds, it overjoyed her to see how much they had in common where it counts.

Over lunch, the subject of Chicago and Dark Hall came up again. John held her hand from across the table. "I'm proud of how well you depended on your intuition and observation skills for handling that bizarre situation."

His praise made her blush.

"You may have to give up your job as a court stenographer and begin a new career as a private investigator."

She rolled her eyes in jest. "There's a lot more for me to learn about being a detective before I could think about quitting my job. But I do appreciate your confidence in me."

That evening, John arrived promptly at six o'clock. "Your carriage awaits," he said, when she opened the door. He directed her attention to the luxury car parked at the curb. Briony's jaw dropped. It was a beautiful silver Cadillac with tail fins and a stainless steel roof.

"That's an Eldorado Brougham. Only four hundred of those babies have been made and they're hand built. I found one right here in Wichita to rent for the night. You deserve the best."

"Oh, John, I feel like Cinderella. I've never ridden in such a fancy car."

"Neither have I," he chuckled. "But I wanted tonight to be special. It's our first real date."

"That's so thoughtful of you." She welcomed him out of the cold. "Come inside and I'll get my wrap."

"Are you hungry?" he asked.

"Famished. I'll be just a minute then we can go." Before she turned, her gaze subtlety raked over him. Under his winter coat, he wore slacks and dress shoes. His hair was soft and shiny, and his face clean-shaven. The masculine scent that lightly wafted off him was intoxicating. Dressed for a romantic night out, he was more handsome than ever.

She felt his heated gaze between her shoulder blades as she reached into the coat closet for her swing coat.

"You look beautiful, Briony." His deep voice

drew her attention. She couldn't help but smile when his eyes roamed over her figure before helping her into the coat. To celebrate the evening, she'd chosen to wear a mid-calf length red dress with a full skirt, a scooped neck, and fitted waist. Since flats were as popular as heels, and the walks were still slushy from recent snowfall, she opted for red flats. A beret hat and clutch completed her ensemble. She hoped to make an impression with her outfit. From the expression in his passion-clouded eyes, her mission had been accomplished.

"We're going now, Mom," she called.

Her mother stepped out of the kitchen wiping her hands on a tea towel. "Hello, John. Nice to see you again."

"Hello, Mrs. Martin. Happy Valentine's day." He presented her with a single long-stemmed rose that Briony hadn't noticed hidden behind his back. Her mother's hand fluttered to her heart, and her face opened into a bright smile Briony hadn't seen in years.

"Thank you, John. How kind of you. I'll put this in a bud vase right away. You kids have a good time tonight."

"We will, Mrs. Martin," he answered.

"Good night, Mom." Briony felt the clasp of John's strong hand once they were outside. She smiled as he escorted her to the Cadillac. "I didn't have any idea you were so charming," she said, as he helped her into the car and shut the door.

"If you're Cinderella, I must be your prince." He winked. "And the evening has just begun."

With directions given to him by the man he rented the Cadillac from, John drove them to the eight-story

Broadview Hotel downtown. Briony knew there was a nice restaurant inside, but she'd never been to it before. "I've always wanted to see inside this hotel. It's supposed to be beautiful. And there's a rooftop garden where people eat in the summer," she told him as he parked the car.

He took her hand and helped her from the car. "Maybe we can eat up there together sometime."

Her eyebrow arched. That comment meant he was planning another visit.

The interior of the hotel was just as magnificent as she'd heard, and the restaurant itself was elegantly decorated for Valentine's Day. Glass vases of red roses sat in the middle of each table, and a man in a tuxedo played romantic tunes on a piano sitting on an elevated stage. Due to all the mouth-watering items on the menu, she had a difficult time deciding what to order.

"Order whatever your heart desires," John said. "I want this night to be perfect. I'm going to have a steak."

After lively conversation and a delicious meal, they each had a dessert of chocolate mousse with fresh whipped cream and strawberries. When Briony thought the night couldn't get any better, John retrieved a small box from the inside pocket of his jacket. It was wrapped in shiny red paper and tied with a silver bow. When he gently placed it in her hand, she nibbled her lip.

"What's this?" she asked.

"One of your presents from me. Open it."

Her fingers trembled as she flicked the ribbon and tore the paper. When she lifted the lid of a small blue suede box, a necklace with a gold pendant shaped in a heart with tiny diamonds around the edges stared at her. "John, it's beautiful!"

To surprise her even further, he rose from his chair and removed the necklace from the box and placed it around her neck. When his fingers grazed her throat, shivers raced through her body. "Thank you," she said, as he returned to his seat. "I'll always treasure it."

"You're welcome. But that's not all. I have one more surprise for you."

She couldn't imagine more. "You're spoiling me. Spending this evening with you is more than I ever dreamed of."

"Well, I want you to spoil you more. And I want you to dream bigger, Briony." He slid an envelope across the table.

Her head tilted.

"Go ahead," he urged.

Her finger slipped under the flap. When she stared at the airline ticket inside, her eyes enlarged.

John grinned. "Right before I left Maine, I took on a new client. I received a phone call from an old friend of my mother's. Seems she's got a mystery needing solved in Savannah, Georgia. I'd like you to go with me and help me solve it."

Speechless, she inhaled several deep breaths, like she always did when she became nervous.

So many questions raced through her mind. What would her mother say? John had won her over, but that didn't mean she'd accept her daughter traipsing around the south with him unmarried. And how could she quit her job? She loved being a court stenographer. Her independence and confidence had grown due to her career.

As if reading her mind, John said, "We can be partners, Briony. Expenses for this case are being paid by my client. We'll split the fee I'm getting. I know it'll be a big sacrifice for you to leave your job. But I really think we have something great starting between us. I don't want to lose it."

"I don't either." She cared for John more than she'd cared for any other man. But it was difficult for her to step out of her comfort zone. Was she strong enough to take such a leap of faith?

When his mouth tipped in a crooked smile, her heart twisted with longing.

"It would be a real adventure," he promised, moving to her side and kneeling next to her. He cupped her hands in his. "We only have one life to live. Let's live it together, right here, right now."

She thought of Ben and how his young life had been cut short. And how her mother had wasted so much of hers bitter and angry.

"What do you say, Briony? Take a chance and go with me to Georgia?"

She stared into John's twinkling eyes and then kissed him in front of whoever was watching in the restaurant. "Yes!" she answered. "How soon do we leave?"

ABOUT THE AUTHOR

Stacey Coverstone is a multi-published author of mysteries, Gothics, contemporary and historical western romance, romantic suspense, and ghost stories. She lives in rural Maryland with her husband and their dogs, cats, and a paint horse named Bill. They have two grown daughters and a baby granddaughter. When she isn't writing a new story or spending time with her family, Stacey enjoys reading, target shooting, photography, traveling, and making scrapbooks of her adventures.

Deception at Dark Hall is Book Two of The Briony Martin Mystery Series.
Cries in the Mist, Book One of the series can be found on Kindle and in paperback from CreateSpace: www.createspace.com/4064483
Watch for Book Three of the series in the coming months.

Please visit Stacey's website for blurbs and excerpts of all her books, as well as purchasing information. You can also join her Announce Only Newsletter if you'd like to be notified when a new book releases:
www.staceycoverstone.com

NOTE: In this novella, *Deception at Dark Hall*, the author has taken creative license with regard to the release date of the movie, *The Three Faces of Eve*, in order to make it work for this story.

Made in United States
Cleveland, OH
19 November 2025

26306464R00075